ARROW OF DESIRE

Handsome and wealthy bachelors are always fair game for ambitious women, and Spenser, Earl of Cleveland, was more eligible than most. He could not be convinced that any woman looked beyond his title, and his refusal to accept the existence of love was an impenetrable armour. He was in need of an heir and therefore must marry, and it was easy to compile a list of suitable brides. But the swift arrow of desire played unexpected havoc with his plans.

JULIET GRAY

ARROW OF DESIRE

Complete and Unabridged

LINFORD
Leicester

First published in Great Britain

First Linford Edition
published 1996

British Library CIP Data

Gray, Juliet
    Arrow of desire.—Large print ed.—
Linford romance library
I. Title II. Series
823.914 [F]

ISBN 0–7089–7837–1

Published by
F. A. Thorpe (Publishing) Ltd.
Anstey, Leicestershire

Set by Words & Graphics Ltd.
Anstey, Leicestershire
Printed and bound in Great Britain by
T. J. Press (Padstow) Ltd., Padstow, Cornwall

This book is printed on acid-free paper

1

SPENSER did not like parties . . . least of all his sister's parties which were too noisy, too exuberant and too unconventional for his taste.

Arriving without warning one pleasant spring evening at his sister's house, he was admitted and warmly greeted by a smiling and slightly intoxicated stranger. Not wishing to become involved, Spenser decided on a quick retreat and was about to leave a message for Victoria when he heard his name. He turned towards his brother-in-law with a smile that held a hint of rueful resignation.

Luke Cardigan greeted him with warmth and unmistakable relief . . . and Spenser knew that he had no hope of immediate escape. He accepted a drink and then, as Luke went in

1

search of his temporarily missing wife, Spenser stood alone, a tall, broad-shouldered and exceptionally attractive man.

It seemed to him that Victoria had acquired some very odd friends whose clothes and manners might be the height of fashion but seemed to him to be ridiculously extrovert and not at all attractive. Perhaps he was out of touch with current trends but he preferred a man to look masculine and a woman to look feminine!

Victoria made her way across the crowded room towards him, looking unmistakably feminine and very beautiful in a filmy dress of silver-grey chiffon, her copper-coloured hair massed high on her head, her blue eyes as dark and magnificent as the sapphire she wore on her left hand. She held out both hands to her brother, smiling with mingled affection and amused astonishment in her lovely eyes. "I don't believe it!" she declared mockingly. "What brings *you* to town? Something very important to

2

lure you away from Staples, surely?"

Spenser clasped her hands and bent to kiss the smooth cheek, smiling . . . the warm and very attractive smile that yet held the merest hint of bored cynicism. "I've heard such tales about you that I came to find out if they are true," he told her lightly.

Victoria wrinkled her shapely nose. "I'm enjoying life if that's what you mean," she said with a touch of defiance. "I suppose some disapproving old tabby has been gossiping over the tea-cups with her cronies about my 'goings-on'?"

"You do seem to be making a name for yourself just lately," he pointed out, a little dryly.

She shrugged her slim shoulders. "Perhaps I am . . . but if Luke doesn't object then I'm sure that no one else has the right to criticise."

Spenser raised a quizzical eyebrow. "And certainly not a mere brother," he agreed wryly.

Victoria laughed. "Oh, you haven't come up from Staples to criticise me . . . or even to concern yourself with my behaviour, I know. What does bring you? Something that will keep you in town for a few weeks, I hope!"

"Oh, I expect to be home again at the end of the week," he told her smoothly. "Business brings me to town . . . and a natural desire to see you and Luke. You look very well, Victoria."

"Oh, marriage agrees with me," she said flippantly. "Where is Luke, anyway . . . does he know that you are here?"

"He is looking for you, I believe. He wandered off a few moments ago." He added mockingly: "He found me in the hall and insisted that I should enjoy myself if I would only put my mind to it."

Victoria smiled . . . but absently for as she glanced about the crowded room for her husband she had caught sight of someone else — and her heart had turned over unexpectedly. She had hoped that he would come to the party

4

but had doubted that he would . . . and now her only thought was to cross the room to be with him. "Poor Spenser . . . you don't care for my parties, do you," she said carelessly. "But don't run away . . . there are some interesting people here and I'm sure you know some of my guests. Do the pretty while I circulate, there's an angel . . . !"

She left him . . . but not to circulate, Spenser suspected. She made her way through the crush of people, resisting all attempts to detain her, until she reached the far corner of the large room and the man who had attracted her attention. Spenser watched with that faint frown touching his eyes as his sister slipped a hand into the man's arm and smiled up at him with a caressing warmth. He thought that he was beginning to understand why the breath of scandal had touched a bride of only six months . . . and he wondered if Luke was truly the complaisant husband that Victoria claimed.

Luke had not returned . . . looking

about him, Spenser knew that most of his sister's guests were people he did not know and felt that he did not care to know. It was typical of Victoria to wander off in that careless fashion without bothering to introduce him to his neighbours . . .

He was attracting notice and he knew it . . . but he was inured to being the focus of attention. Without conceit, he appreciated that his height, his impressive build, his good looks and the famous red hair of the Chadwicks with its distinctive white blaze was sufficient to attract notice without the added interest of his title and the wealth that went with it. And he did not doubt that his identity was known to almost everyone in the room.

No one approached him. Spenser was not aware that he looked quite unapproachable, that there was a faint hauteur in his expression and that his dislike of the company in which he found himself was sufficiently evident to deter strangers from introducing themselves. He was a proud man and life had taught him to be cynical. Knowing the universal love of a title, he frequently suspected the friendly overtures of strangers — just as he mistrusted the blatant interest of women who contrived to cast out lures in his direction.

He was an eligible bachelor and fair game for optimistic mothers and their ambitious daughters. Sometimes it amused him that he had only to enter into a mild flirtation for the world to assume that he meant to marry at last . . . more often it bored and irritated him. He knew that he was considered to be cold, heartless and impossible to please. But he had yet to be convinced that a woman cared for him rather than for the title and the social standing that he might bestow on her. Years of transparent pursuit had made him a cynic . . . and having never fallen in love with any woman he felt that at thirty-four he was rather too old for the folly. But he must marry . . . it was his duty to provide an heir to the title and estates. Love on either side need not enter into the contract . . . and he meant to make his choice with a cool, clear head and a heart unaffected by the emotions that made fools of so many men.

Cold-blooded but practical . . . and Spenser, Earl of Cleveland was a very practical and level-headed man with a strong sense of duty and a fierce pride in his family traditions of honour and integrity and loyalty. Marriage for a Chadwick was not to be entered into lightly. As he must marry then he meant to marry a woman who knew and understood the terms of the marriage he proposed . . . a woman of birth and breeding, preferably attractive and intelligent, possessing poise and good taste and personality, a woman who would bring both grace and dignity to her role as his countess . . .

An apologetic Luke reached his side and Spenser dragged his thoughts back to the present.

"Not much in your line . . . this kind of thing, I'm afraid," Luke said easily. "Nor mine, if I am honest about it," he added with a faintly rueful smile.

"But the breath of life to Victoria," Spenser commented dryly.

Luke nodded. "She loves it all . . . she set out to outdo every other hostess in town and she has succeeded," he said, a little proudly. "The good, the bad and the beautiful . . . you can meet them all here at some time or another. All levels of society attend Victoria's parties . . . writers, actors, artists, film stars and pop singers, university dons and street buskers, near-royalty and East Enders." He gave a wry laugh. "Victoria's parties are all the rage. Name any celebrity you choose . . . she'll contrive that you meet in this house before you leave town. I've met more celebrities in six months than I ever knew to exist!"

"Which particular celebrity is occupying her attention just now?" Spenser asked lightly.

Luke's glance unerringly found his wife in the midst of a crowd. "You don't know him . . . ? Julius Marlowe, the photographer."

"I know *of* him . . . " The faint emphasis was unmistakably contemptuous.

Luke's expression held a slight wariness. "His reputation, you mean . . . who doesn't? It isn't very savoury, I agree. But Victoria won't come to any harm. She's very level-headed, you know."

Spenser raised an eyebrow in faint surprise. In all the twenty-three years of her existence, he had never considered his sister to be particularly level-headed. She was incurably impulsive, hopelessly spoiled, strong-willed . . . and utterly enchanting. He had not been surprised when Luke Cardigan fell heavily in love with Victoria . . . but he had been astonished that his fickle and flirtatious sister had chosen to marry a quiet and unassuming young American whom he had expected to bore her within weeks. It seemed that he had been right . . . Victoria *was* bored with her devoted, patient and apparently uncomplaining husband and had soon sought diversion and amusement in other directions.

He had little faith in her discretion but he did not believe that his sister, brought up in the proud tradition of duty to one's family name, would be actively unfaithful to her husband or would bring herself to the divorce courts. A Chadwick might regret her marriage but she would make the best of it . . . an inflexible rule that owed as much to self-respect as to family pride. Victoria was merely enjoying herself — as anyone who knew her might have expected when she married a man who, for all his excellent qualities, could scarcely be described as exciting . . . as anything but dull if one cared to be candid!

"I imagine that you won't allow her to come to any harm," he returned levelly and hoped that he was not indulging optimism too far. For he had yet to discover that Luke was sufficiently forceful to prevent his lovely wife from doing whatever she wished. In six months, it seemed that she had contrived to fill the house with a host of people that he obviously did not care for, had no doubt exploited her natural extravagance to the full and had managed to become very much talked about as a bored and discontented wife who was ready to enjoy a light-hearted affair with any man who caught her fickle fancy . . . and apparently Luke had not made the least attempt to assert his authority as her husband.

Spenser believed that his sister needed a firm and capable hand on her rein, like all women . . . she might be hard to hold at first but she would soon settle down and learn to respect an authority she had never known in the past. She might even learn to love the man she had married, he thought wryly.

Luke's mouth tightened just a

fraction. "No, I won't allow that," he said quietly, almost grimly. Then his expression softened as he glanced once more at his beautiful, vivacious wife. "You have heard some of the gossip, I imagine," he went on smoothly. "But you needn't be anxious . . . Victoria enjoys playing with fire but she won't burn her fingers." He smiled suddenly. "She is very practised in the art of flirtation, you know."

Spenser agreed, a little dryly. He did not share Luke's comfortable confidence that Victoria was merely flirting with Julius Marlowe. There was a disturbing degree of intimacy in her smile, in the way her hand rested so lightly within his arm, in her easy familiarity with a man who had a dangerous reputation as a womaniser. A brilliant photographer and a society favourite, Marlowe had a long string of dubious affairs to his credit — and a wife who was never produced but whose existence provided the man with an excellent means of escape from any affair that became too hot to handle. Spenser was not at all pleased to learn that his sister counted the man as one of her particular friends . . . but Victoria had warned him against interference and he knew himself powerless to do or say anything if her husband was content to allow the friendship to continue . . .

More punctilious than his wife, Luke ensured that he was introduced to one or two people before he again left him to carry out the various duties of a host . . . but Spenser managed to extricate himself with very little difficulty and, avoiding the eye of those who knew him and wished to talk to him, he made his way towards the open window which led to the terrace and the gardens. The room was uncomfortably overheated and stuffy with tobacco smoke and the mingling of too many heady perfumes . . . he greeted the cool night air on his head with relief although it lacked the sweet freshness of country air.

He was seldom content away from Staples . . . his home and his land were his dearest loves and the conscientious management of the estates was not solely due to duty but was also a reflection of the pride and affection he felt for the acres which surrounded the graceful old house where Chadwicks had lived and died for generations.

He glanced without interest at the girl who turned her head as he stepped out to the terrace, wondered briefly if she had also sought a temporary escape from the party . . . and promptly dismissed her from his mind.

The indifference of his glance froze the friendly smile on her lips . . . and Sophy knew that he had not recognised her. She doubted if he had even seen her in that moment when their eyes met. She felt a stirring of resentment for they were not strangers . . . they had met at Victoria's wedding, even danced together — and she had decided that he was quite the most attractive man she had ever met but insufferably arrogant and impossible to like. He had scarcely spoken to her while they danced and she had gained the impression that he was carrying out an irksome duty and considered her to be very much beneath his notice.

Sophy did not expect any man to be bowled over at first meeting by her looks or personality . . . she knew that she was not distinguished in either respect. But she did expect courtesy and a certain amount of interested attention from a man who was introduced to her at a social function . . . and Spenser Chadwick had failed on both points.

He stood partly in shadow, staring across the moonlit gardens, a tall, powerfully-built man whose good looks held a hint of cold austerity. Sophy studied him with a frank and not at all complimentary appraisal . . . just as she had studied him earlier in the evening and despised him for his obvious boredom and distaste for his company. No one could have doubted the scornful mockery in his eyes as he surveyed his fellow-guests or his disinclination to make himself pleasant to his neighbours.

Sophy had no patience with so much pride . . . for he was a man like any other for all the social and financial advantages he had always enjoyed. Did he really suppose himself to be a cut above the rest of mankind? It certainly seemed that he did — and Sophy regarded him with intense dislike.

Suddenly becoming aware of that steady gaze, Spenser turned his head . . . and was startled to meet such unmistakable hostility in a stranger's eyes. There was a challenge in the very way she stood, her slender body taut and her head held high. Thinking that she had spoken and resented receiving no reply, he said levelly: "I beg your pardon?"

"So you should!" she retorted tartly.

Spenser raised an eyebrow, faintly amused by the indignant retort. "I'm sorry . . . I didn't realise that you had spoken to me," he said lightly.

"But I wouldn't dare do so without formal permission," she returned dryly. "I didn't speak to you . . . one snub is more than enough, I promise you!"

Spenser turned to face her, intrigued and even more amused. "Did I snub you . . . I wasn't aware of it." Seeing her fully for the first time, he added: "We've met before, I believe?"

"I'm flattered that you should remember," Sophy said coldly and with blatant mendacity.

A faint smile flickered about his lips. "I gather that I should not have forgotten. Forgive me . . . my memory is not always reliable."

"Particularly when you have no desire to remember," she suggested coolly.

He was beginning to feel just a faint stirring of irritation. "Perhaps you did not make much of an impression at the time," he suggested with a bluntness that matched her own.

"It isn't easy to penetrate your armour, is it?" Her tone was deceptively sweet . . . her expression was deceptively innocent.

"My . . . armour?" he echoed in surprise.

"I imagine the Earl of Cleveland doesn't allow many people to intrude on his notice . . . no doubt he has to consider his dignity too much."

Spenser stared at her in astonishment . . . and then he began to laugh. She regarded him with dislike but it was wholly impossible for her to ignore that infectious chuckle and a reluctant smile touched her own lips.

He looked at her, his eyes twinkling. "I certainly seem to have outraged *your* dignity in some way . . . what can I do to make amends, I wonder?"

Sophy hesitated, a little surprised to discover that he had almost disarmed her with the charm of his smile, the friendliness of his tone. "That isn't necessary . . . you can't possibly hope to be forgiven, you know," she told him firmly, a smile lurking in her eyes and voice.

"No, but you are compensated by the fact that I am not likely to forget you again," he returned, smiling. "It's a long time since I was put so firmly in my place, you know."

"We must hope that it has done you a great deal of good," she said sweetly. "Goodnight . . . "

Taken aback by her words, he looked after her as she slipped through the open window into the house. Within seconds, he followed her but she had moved so swiftly that there was no sign of her in the crowded room . . . and he was immediately claimed by a late-comer to the party who greeted him with surprise and the easy familiarity of long friendship.

Tall, slender, dark-haired and sophisticated, Georgina Winslow was the daughter of an able politician, the grand-daughter of an earl . . . and she had been first brought to Spenser's notice when she was barely seventeen, more than ten years before. They had enjoyed a brief flirtation before her capricious affections had been transferred to another man and they had continued to be friends who liked and understood each other very well. Having hoped to see her while he was in town, Spenser was pleased by this chance meeting . . . and interested observers noticed the warmth which touched his rather austere features as he looked down at the beautiful Georgina.

"This is a delightful surprise," she said lightly, confidently. "Victoria didn't tell me that you were expected tonight."

"I am a delightful surprise to Victoria, too," he assured her, smiling. She came high on the list as a possible bride for she had all the qualities he wanted in his wife. But he did not know if she would be willing to marry him. He might exert all his charm and still discover that she preferred her freedom to the undeniable restrictions of marriage . . .

In fact, Georgina had every intention of marrying Spenser Chadwick . . . it had been in her mind for a very long time although she had never allowed him to know it. "I'm surprised that you didn't turn tail and run when you found yourself involved in a party," she said lightly. "When did you come up to town?"

"This afternoon."

She looked up at him with faint amusement in her eyes. "And how long do you stay?"

"Only for a few days."

She nodded. "At least your friends will see something of you, Spenser . . . if only for a few days. You are almost a stranger."

"We could never be strangers," he said softly and with meaning.

She smiled up at him. "It's months since we met," she reminded him with faint reproach.

"Then we must make up for lost time," he said promptly. "Dine with me tomorrow?"

Georgina laughed. "If I'm free," she returned provocatively. She was gratified that he wished for her company . . . at the same time, one never really knew if Spenser was merely being courteous. There were times when she wished he were a little more transparent for he never seemed to reveal his true thoughts and feelings.

For years she had felt that she had a prior claim to his affections and attentions because of that early flirtation and their continued friendship but he seldom encouraged her to suppose that it was true. Nevertheless she was quite convinced that he felt a fondness for her that no other woman enjoyed and that he would have married her long ago if she had not temporarily lost interest in him when another man appeared briefly more attractive. She believed that Spenser had never wholly forgiven her for the desertion — but could easily be persuaded to do so if and when she chose.

He had been very attentive at Victoria's wedding and she had been confident that if she had chosen to exert her charms to the full he would have followed up the encouragement she offered and very likely fallen wholeheartedly in love with her. She had discovered at an early age that men were apt to fall in love with her, however fleetingly, and she had enjoyed a succession of light-hearted affairs without committing herself to a lasting or too demanding relationship with any man.

She did not believe that Spenser was incapable of loving, as so many people claimed. Like herself, he was merely reluctant to exchange his freedom for the bondage of marriage . . . and no doubt he had disciplined his emotions to avoid the mistake of falling in love with a totally unsuitable woman. In his position, he could not marry where he pleased . . . his bride must be chosen with a view to the rôle she must play as his countess. Georgina knew herself to be an eligible choice and although she was not at all in love with Spenser it would suit her very well to be his wife . . . not just yet, perhaps, but in the not-too-distant future . . .

Talking to her, dancing with her, Spenser wondered what was lacking in him that he could be so unmoved by Georgina's undeniable beauty and warm femininity, the appeal that she seemed to have for most men. It was impossible not to like a woman he had known for so long . . . equally impossible not to admire her elegance and self-possession and beauty of face and figure. Yet the woman did not seem to exist who did not bore him within a very short time of making her acquaintance . . . and he had known Georgina for a very long time.

She was attractive, intelligent, sophisticated, a woman of the world, possessed of all the qualities he wanted in a wife . . . but he could not discover in himself the slightest desire to marry her. She might be wholly eligible but he was chilled by the thought of marriage with a woman who meant so little to him and who so obviously regarded him with no more than mild and probably habitual affection.

He had never loved any woman and he knew that no woman had ever loved him. But he felt that something more than mere liking and long association was necessary to a successful marriage. He did not wish to marry at all but it was time that he took a wife and acquired an heir. He could not cross Georgina off his list simply because he was in no mood to appreciate her attractions . . . among the women he had in mind, he felt that she was still the only one he could bring himself to marry. He knew her well, for one thing . . . and he could trust her to know and abide by the terms of the marriage he proposed. There would be no risk that Georgina would indulge in casual affairs or behave in any way that might expose her to public comment. She would know and accept exactly what was expected of her as his wife and she would not give him a moment's anxiety. She would make an excellent mistress for Staples, a charming and delightful hostess, a dutiful wife and mother . . . and she would make very few demands on him which was surely what he wanted in the woman he married.

It was foolish sentiment to wish that he could contemplate his inevitable marriage with delight. He had always known that he must make a suitable and practical marriage . . . and what could be more suitable or practical than marrying a woman like Georgina? Love was all very well for those who believed in it . . . he did not. He had managed without love in the past and would not mourn its absence in the future. For it seemed to him that affection and understanding and mutual trust were more reliable and a very much better basis for any marriage than the ephemeral fantasy of love . . .

2

GEORGINA had arrived with an escort in tow and Spenser could not monopolise her attention even if he had wished. He did not wish it for it was no part of his plan to set tongues in motion at this juncture. It suited him very well that she had called in only briefly before going on to a nightclub — and if she had imagined that he might try to persuade her to stay longer she was doomed to disappointment. But she had the satisfaction of having his invitation to dinner for the following night.

People were constantly arriving and departing — it was that kind of affair. So it was scarcely surprising that Spenser sought in vain for the girl who had intrigued him on the terrace. An unusual girl . . . he wished he could remember when and where they had met before. He could not recall her name, knew nothing about her except that she was young and slight and possessed an impulsive tongue. The recollection of all she had said amused him . . . no, he was not likely to forget her a second time. He had liked her despite that rampant hostility . . . and her dry sense of humour was very much to his taste. He might have suspected a deliberate provocation to attract his interest if she had not left him so abruptly . . . as it was, he rather thought that she disliked him and did not mean to conceal the fact.

Victoria finally managed to tear herself away from Marlowe. She skimmed towards him with every indication that she was dancing on air. Vibrantly beautiful, radiantly youthful, she looked very well pleased with herself . . . and Spenser felt like slapping her for such careless disregard for her husband's feelings and the censure of her guests. He almost wished it was his practice to interfere with the way his sister ran her life . . . but he had found it difficult to cope with a headstrong girl so much younger than himself and in the past she had always contrived to extricate herself from scrapes without his assistance.

"Enjoying yourself, darling?" she asked blithely.

"Not particularly," he told her bluntly.

She laughed, not at all offended. "Doesn't anyone interest you? You always were so hard to please! Didn't I see you talking to Georgina Winslow a few moments ago?"

"She is just leaving," he pointed out.

Victoria followed the direction of his gaze. "Oh yes . . . I hope the party isn't breaking up so soon. They are looking for me, aren't they . . . ? Excuse me . . . !"

He looked after her with some impatience . . . and decided that the popularity of her parties must be due to the fact that she made little attempt to influence her guests' enjoyment and allowed them to treat her house very much like a club where they might meet their particular friends and say and do exactly as they wished.

Georgina's departure certainly seemed to have a signal effect on others. Gradually the crowd dwindled to a mere handful . . . among them, Julius Marlowe who seemed curiously indifferent to Victoria's blatant interest while doing nothing to discourage it. While he remained, Victoria was gay, vivacious, bubbling with spirits . . . when he went the change in her was so marked that it influenced the decision of those who still lingered to make their farewells. All her effervescence had vanished . . . her vivacity was obviously forced and Spenser felt that there was a defiant awareness of guilt in her change of mood.

She returned from seeing the last of her guests from the house . . . and surveyed the chaos caused by a most successful party with a rueful expression.

31

It was not the end of the evening as far as she was concerned. She had every hope of persuading Luke to take her out to dine and dance at a nightclub . . . and no inclination whatsoever to go tamely to bed while the night was still young.

She had forgotten her brother and was not aware of his presence in the high-winged armchair as she turned to Luke who was sorting and stacking records into neat piles. Warily, a little apprehensive, she said brightly: "It was fun, don't you think? Are you tired . . . I'm not! Shall we go to the *Caprice* . . . I could dance all night!"

Luke wished he could be angry, could resist the melting appeal in those lovely eyes . . . but she was such a child for all her sophistication and it was impossible to believe that her behaviour was due to anything but thoughtlessness and a single-minded zest for enjoyment. He went to her and drew her towards him with hands on her slim shoulders. "Don't you think it might be pleasant to stay home tonight . . . we seem to have so little time to ourselves, Victoria."

Exclaiming, she slipped from the gentle restraint of his hands. "Spenser! When did he slip away? I particularly asked him to stay . . . !"

Her brother rose reluctantly from the deep chair whose high wings had concealed him from their view . . . he had been enjoying those few moments of welcome quiet and relaxation. "I'm still here," he said dryly. "A *very* successful party, Victoria . . . I thought your friends meant to make a night of it."

She laughed. "You're a social misfit, my dear . . . how can you dislike parties? It isn't at all kind of you, Spenser — no one is ever bored at *my* parties!"

"You must allow me to be the exception," he drawled. "No doubt everyone else had a marvellous time." He glanced at Luke with a faintly sardonic gleam in his eyes and his brother-in-law smiled in rueful response.

"I'm afraid I should also be a social misfit if Victoria would allow it," he said lightly. "A quiet evening at home with my wife would be much more to my liking on many occasions."

Victoria glanced at him reproachfully, a silent reminder of the quiet evenings which had proved to be so unsatisfactory to them both of late.

"No doubt . . . but you would find such evenings very dull, I promise you," she said tautly, a brittle flippancy in her tone. "I like to have people about me, Luke . . . you knew that when you married me. I'm spoiled and selfish and I make life miserable for everyone when I'm not allowed to have my own way." There was a rancour behind the words that informed Spenser that she taunted her husband with something unwisely uttered in anger. "You wouldn't be at all happy if I gave up parties and all my friends to please you."

A retort was obviously quivering on Luke's lips . . . Spenser suspected that only his presence checked its utterance. He intervened pleasantly: "If you mean to finish the night at the *Caprice* I wish you had warned me of it, Victoria . . . I might have been in my bed an hour ago!"

"Oh, it was just an impulse," she retorted petulantly. "Luke hates nightclubs . . . don't you, darling? I daren't insist on dragging him out when he has suffered an evening of my friends without a word of complaint." Her tone was mocking and almost contemptuous. She threw herself into an armchair and took a cigarette from the box on the low table by her side. Luke moved swiftly to give her a light . . . she bent her lovely head over the flame of his lighter and thanked him with a careless, unsmiling nod and an expression in her eyes that made Spenser itch once again to slap her.

He wondered if she often treated Luke to that petulant bitchiness and why the magic had fled from a marriage which was still in its infancy? What could have gone wrong? He had supposed Luke to be too deeply in love for his feelings to undergo change when he was no longer so blind to Victoria's faults and follies. And why did he allow her to treat him with so little respect and consideration, exposing him to humiliation? And what had happened to the sweetness and generosity and warmly affectionate nature that had always distinguished Victoria for all her faults?

Victoria smiled suddenly . . . but the smile was meant for her brother rather than for the hovering Luke. "Now your news, darling," she said lightly. "Why *are* you in town?"

"I told you . . . I came up on business."

"What kind of business, though?" she persisted.

"Oh, mainly tax affairs," he returned smoothly.

She studied him thoughtfully. "Is anything wrong . . . money matters, I mean? I know you've been pouring money into the estate for years and you once told me that it would be a long time before the investment yielded any return. It must cost a great deal to run Staples. If you need money . . . well, Luke would be only too pleased to help, you know," she finished rather diffidently.

Luke nodded his agreement. "Certainly! Any time . . . Spenser knows that, of course."

"Thank you . . . I appreciate the offer. But money is no problem, fortunately. The estate has been yielding considerable returns for some years now — and since you married my extravagant sister and took over her many bills my bank balance has been remarkably healthy," he added, smiling.

Victoria laughed, her good humour rapidly returning. "At least Luke doesn't scold me for running up bills," she retorted. "You have a very mean streak, my dear brother."

He was not offended. His eyes

twinkled as he said: "I am mean and you are hopelessly extravagant . . . the truth must lie somewhere between the two. I believe that *my* wife will never have cause to complain of my lack of generosity."

Victoria's eyes widened abruptly. "Spenser! Are you going to be married? Is that why you are in town?"

Luke looked at his brother-in-law with faint surprise . . . like everyone else he had assumed that Spenser was indifferent to the thought of marriage.

Spenser shrugged. "You know that I must marry . . . it's been hanging over my head for years."

"Yes, of course . . . but who is she?" Victoria demanded impatiently.

Spenser leaned back in his chair and regarded his sister with a smile in his grey eyes. "I haven't yet decided . . . I thought you might care to advise me," he said carelessly.

"Advise you . . . ?" she echoed in astonishment.

Spenser studied the glowing tip of his

cigarette with a deliberate nonchalance. "There are three or four women on my list . . . any one of them suitable for my purpose. I must have an heir — therefore I must have a wife. Georgina . . . ? She's very attractive and I've known her for a long time. Sarah Markham? She would most certainly bequeath the Markham nose to our children, I'm afraid. Alice Maynard has much to recommend her including the land which runs parallel to my own . . . you don't think her passion for horses would become an intolerable bore? I might marry Susan Wingate . . . she's very pretty and good-natured and I suppose one could get used to that irritating laugh in time. I would include Jocelyn Welch but I doubt if the family needs any more red hair or the temper that goes with it. What do you say, my children . . . which of them shall I marry? I'm really finding it very difficult to decide, you know."

Victoria was speechless . . . so rare in his experience of his sister that laughter lurked in his eyes as he regarded her incredulous face. He glanced towards Luke with a faintly raised eyebrow and an enquiring smile. That usually quiet-spoken young man said vehemently: "Not one of them, of course . . . if you are really interested in my opinion!"

Spenser smiled deprecatingly. "But I must marry, Luke . . . I thought you understood my position."

"There's plenty of time, I imagine," Luke retorted dryly.

"But one can never be sure," he said smoothly. "My present heir is a distant cousin in Canada who has no interest in Staples . . . and I'm sure he has neither wish nor expectation of inheriting the title. The matter is beginning to weigh heavy on my conscience . . . and I am also just a little weary of eligible bachelorhood."

Victoria found her voice. "You have to be joking, Spenser," she said slowly but she knew that he was very much in earnest. For all the lightness of his tone and manner there was an air of resolution about him . . . and she knew how inflexible he could be in matters that affected his strong sense of duty. "Even if you are serious, how can you be so sure that any one of those women will marry you simply for the asking?"

Spenser smiled. It was a cynical, mocking little smile. "Which of them will refuse me, do you suppose?" he asked with a hint of bitterness.

She was on the point of assuring him that no woman would accept such a cold-blooded proposition when she realised the truth of his words. He was handsome, well-born, wealthy . . . many women would leap at the chance of becoming his wife. Georgina would not hesitate and would certainly not look for love in such a marriage. Sarah Markham would leap at a proposal from any eligible man. Alice Maynard was the daughter of his immediate neighbours and marriage with Spenser would delight her family and please her very well . . . his thoroughbred horses and well-run stables would attract her more than the man and it was unlikely that she would give much thought to the demands of marriage as long as she could indulge in her passion for horses to the full. Susan Wingate had fancied herself in love with Spenser for years . . . .

"I wish I could scoff at your conceit," she said ruefully. "But I can't . . . you're so right. Any one of them would marry you without hesitation."

His lips twisted wryly. "It isn't conceit . . . heaven knows I've learned to be humble about my attraction for women. Do you think it pleases me to know that virtually any woman of my acquaintance would take me for a husband . . . not for my own charms but because I am who I am?"

Victoria leaned forward and cradled her chin in her hands. "Well, if you are serious — and I agree that you've named the only eligibles — then I think that Georgina is your best bet," she said seriously.

Spenser nodded. "I've reached the same conclusion, more or less. But she may need persuading — she likes her freedom, you know."

Luke looked from one to the other in irritated astonishment. "Victoria, don't encourage your brother in this absurdity," he said stiffly. "What happiness or satisfaction can he hope to find in such a marriage?"

"I'm only concerned with acquiring an heir," Spenser said carelessly. "I'm not a marrying man by nature. All I want is a wife with a certain amount of affection for me and whose birth and breeding makes her acceptable as my countess in the eyes of the world. Forgive me . . . but you cannot be expected to appreciate that a man in my position may not marry just anyone who takes his fancy."

"Why not?" Luke demanded a little belligerently. "Why shouldn't you marry a shop assistant or a typist? Does your wife have to be a Georgina Winslow or an Alice Maynard? Who raised an eyebrow when your sister married me . . . my grandfather was a Polish tailor and my father made his money from the manufacture of soap and disinfectants! Come on now, Spenser . . . you're living in the past!"

"Oh, that's different!" Victoria exclaimed impatiently. "Of course you don't understand . . . how could you? Chadwicks don't marry shop assistants — or even fall in love with them!"

Luke looked at her with rare coldness. "Do they ever go out of their way to meet them?" he asked tautly. "It seems to me that some of your aristocratic families could do with a little healthy peasant blood now and again."

Spenser chuckled. "If I knew a healthy peasant who didn't give a snap of her fingers for my title I'd marry her, Luke. But the crux of the matter is that class distinction exists whether we like it or not . . . and it works both ways, you know. It's a way of life not a barrier that can be knocked down overnight. A shop assistant wouldn't be happy as my countess . . . it would make too many demands on her, be too much of a strain. One has to be bred to these things . . . and very few people are happy outside their natural environment. Send Victoria out to work as a typist and she will never be anything but the daughter of an earl at heart. Take a working-class girl and make her a countess and she will fret for her own kind, the way of life that she knows and understands, the comfort and security of being herself in surroundings where she feels at home. It isn't snobbery, Luke . . . it's common-sense. I don't doubt that in time we shall be a classless society but I'm afraid that I cannot wait that long for my heir," he finished lightly.

Luke had listened in courteous silence. Now he said slowly: "I see your point, of course. Similarity of background must always be an advantage in marriage." Suddenly he grinned. "But I'm curious to know what you would do if you fell in love with a working-class girl, Spenser?"

"Fall promptly out of love," he replied carelessly. "I'm told that love can overcome all obstacles but I'm afraid I should always feel that the family portraits were reproaching me. But the situation isn't likely to arise, of course . . . I'm past the age of falling in love." He laughed lightly. "I'm a practical man and I mean to make a practical marriage . . ."

Truly feminine, Victoria was appalled to hear her brother declare that he was past falling in love. She had long regretted the cynicism and the boredom which had become so marked in his outlook but she had always clung to the belief that it would be erased when he met a woman he could love and who would love him in his own right. The marriage he contemplated would set him beyond the chance of happiness that could transform his life and turn him into a very different man. She loved him dearly but she deplored the innate practicality of outlook that bestowed a certain hardness on his heart.

Succeeding to the title before he was twenty, constantly pursued by women since he had reached maturity, never lacking for friends whatever their motives in acquiring his friendship, Spenser had been thoroughly spoiled and his cynical attitude to life and people had been the inevitable outcome. He had become rapidly bored with the social round, the inevitable monotony of meeting the same people in the same places at the same time of year . . . and there was no novelty for Spenser in meeting new people whose approach and attitude were invariably similar to that of everyone he met.

He was her brother and she sympathised with his feelings throughout the years. But the age gap between them was considerable and she had never known or understood him as well as she could have wished. She wanted to believe that he was a warm, tender and very ardent man beneath the

cold and cynical exterior but she
had never found much evidence of
such qualities. He was affectionate and
indulgent towards her and he had never
attempted to thwart her or advise her
against doing what she wished to do
. . . Victoria knew that his careless
attitude sprang from indifference. It
was not the indifference born of lack
of affection but the indifference of
a man who had cultivated a cold
reserve to protect the vulnerability of
his nature. She doubted if he was still
vulnerable . . . his reserve had become
second nature and, like everyone else,
she doubted if the armour about his
heart could be penetrated by anyone
in the world.

She felt a great compassion for him.
Loving was a painful and demanding
experience and it had brought her
disillusion and disappointment but she
still believed that it was a vital necessity
to the fulfilment of every man and
woman. Spenser had never loved, it
seemed — and in her view he suffered

an emptiness in his life, a bleakness of spirit. She did not regret the love that had turned her world upside-down, the love that had brought so brief a happiness, the love she was still so eager and so willing to bestow on a man who did not want it.

She stifled a sigh. Her marriage had been a mistake . . . she did not want Spenser to know the pain and dissatisfaction of a marriage without mutual love. It was obvious that he felt no more than ordinary liking for Georgina and it seemed unlikely that they would learn to love each other after marriage. No doubt they would go their own ways, have their own friends and interests — and all he would ask of Georgina was the heir that he needed. Victoria knew that such an arrangement would be disastrous . . . they would drift apart just as she and Luke had done and end up by scarcely liking and tolerating each other.

Georgina or any other woman who

meant so little to him . . . the result would surely be the same. Yet there was nothing she could do to prevent him making such a marriage . . .

She was silent while the two men talked of world affairs. Suddenly she broke into their conversation with all her habitual impulsiveness; "I don't like it, Spenser! I've nothing against Georgina but isn't there any woman you want to marry, someone you care for if only a little?"

He raised a quizzical eyebrow at this abrupt return to a subject he had adroitly dropped. "I'm afraid there isn't . . . it really doesn't matter to me whom I marry."

She studied him ruefully. "That's a terrible admission, Spenser," she said slowly.

"Is it? It happens to be the truth," he told her lightly. "I can't be the only man in the world who doesn't want a wife, my dear."

"No . . . but it seems very odd to me," she said frankly.

"You are a woman . . . not one of your sex cares to admit that it's possible for a man to be entirely content without a woman in his life," he returned, smiling.

She said grudgingly: "Georgina is fond of you, I suppose . . . and she would be just the kind of wife to suit you. But I wish you would wait, Spenser . . . you don't have to rush into marriage and you might yet meet someone you can love."

He shrugged. "One woman is much like another, surely. I believe it has been said that a man might marry any one of a dozen of a type that suits him and be equally as happy as his nature allows him to be. Marriage may be instinctive for a woman but men are not cast in the same mould, you know," he told her dryly.

"Cynic!" she reproached.

"Circumstances have made me so," he retorted. "Women are opportunists . . . introduce me to a woman who doesn't pretend to admire me when she is really imagining herself as my countess and I'll undertake to marry her!"

"If she would have you!" Victoria said tartly.

He smiled. "If she would have me . . . and if she exists." Suddenly he chuckled and Victoria looked at him with an enquiry in her eyes. "I had a brief encounter this evening with someone who didn't appear to be impressed with my face or my fortune," he explained, his eyes twinkling at the memory of the girl on the terrace.

"Who was that?" Victoria asked quickly, struck by a certain warmth in the retrospective smile that hovered about his lips.

"I've no idea . . . one of your friends, I suppose. I gather that we'd met before and she took exception to my failure to remember the encounter . . . she may have been justified. She left me with the definite impression that a third meeting wouldn't be greeted with cries of delight on her part."

"Describe her!"

He shook his head. "Much too difficult and it really doesn't matter. I've no wish to meet her again. I don't think my ego could survive it." He glanced at his watch. "You are dead on your feet, Victoria . . . and Luke has been wishing me gone for the past half-hour."

Luke shook his head, smiling . . . but he made no attempt to dissuade his brother-in-law from leaving. As they shook hands in warm friendliness, he said quietly: "I hope you won't go through with that suggestion, Spenser . . . I'm convinced it would be a mistake."

"Such marriages are often the most successful — although I can't expect you and Victoria to agree with me, of course. But as a mere onlooker it has seemed to me many times that love is a complication in one's life, you know," he returned smoothly.

"Oh, *our* marriage is entirely successful," Victoria exclaimed with

53

an edge to her voice. "Almost a marriage of convenience in the way that we've agreed not to interfere with each other's pleasures . . . I have my parties and my friends and Luke has his quiet evenings at home with his books and music for the most part. It's working out very well, isn't it, darling?" She threw her husband an unmistakable challenge with the words and the mockery in her tone.

Seeing Luke stiffen and his mouth compress, Spenser said swiftly, lightly: "I expect everyone has their own blueprint for marriage. I shouldn't care to judge the happiness or otherwise of any marriage by outward appearances. The onlooker doesn't always see most of the game."

"The success of any marriage depends on what goes on behind closed doors," Victoria said lightly . . . and sent her brother a smile that was intended to reassure him but merely convinced him that something was very wrong with that particular marriage. He left them with a vague disquiet. Victoria was too proud to seek advice and guidance from any quarter . . . and he fancied that Luke was deliberately blinding himself to the truth of an obvious estrangement . . .

3

LUKE looked down at his young and very lovely wife with a rueful tenderness . . . but Victoria, meeting his gaze with a cool enquiry, saw only reproach and none of the love she had once believed that he felt for her.

She was proud . . . too proud to ask him why his feelings had changed, even to let him know that she was aware of the complacent indifference which had replaced the warm ardour of the man she had married. If he chose to pretend that nothing was wrong between them then she certainly did not mean to bring it out into the open. They were living an intolerable lie . . . but that was better than a complete break with the man she loved.

"Spenser seems to doubt our happiness," he said quietly.

"Why should he?" she returned carelessly. "All the world knows that our marriage is a success."

The irony of her tone did not escape him but he attributed it to her disappointment that marriage was not the ecstatic adventure she had supposed. He accepted that she was disappointed in him, that she found him dull and unexciting and poor company by comparison with her volatile friends, that she was restless and discontented . . . and he did not cease to marvel that she had married him. He did not know, because she skilfully concealed it, that she ached with the longing to know herself loved, yearned for the sweetness and ardour and magic that had touched the early days of their marriage.

Luke would have been horrified to learn that Victoria doubted his love for her . . . it had never occurred to him that the free rein he allowed her might be construed as indifference or lack of desire for her constant presence by his side. From the beginning, he had appreciated that she had always enjoyed her freedom to the full and he had decided that to keep her content he must not attempt to restrict her in any way. Knowing that she was very young and a little wilful, somewhat spoiled by too much attention and admiration, he had felt that she would need more time than most women to adjust to marriage ... and he had uttered no word of protest when it appeared that she expected to live her life very much as she had done before her marriage. Perhaps it had been a mistake but it seemed to be too late to rectify it ... even the least hint of criticism was resented by the girl who had followed her own inclinations for years without check and Luke feared to lose her if he ought to persuade her into a way of life that held no charms for her.

Perhaps she had not been ready for marriage. Certainly he had soon realised that she had married him as the result of an impulsive infatuation, allowing herself no time to be sure of her feelings — and he had been too deeply in love to question the depth or the lasting quality of the emotions he had so amazingly aroused in the lovely and much-admired Victoria Chadwick.

He was a patient man . . . tolerant and kindly, he accepted his wife as she was and supposed that she would eventually settle down and hoped that she would come to love him a little in time. Marriage was still very new to her . . . every couple had their problems in the first months and the necessary adjustment of two separate individuals to living together in such intimacy was no overnight miracle even for the deeply in love.

Victoria stifled a yawn. "I'm tired," she said stiffly. "It's been a hectic evening . . . I think I'll go to bed."

"You would dance all night if I took you to the *Caprice*," Luke said, smiling. He touched her cheek with gentle, caressing fingers. "Shall I take you?" he suggested with the indulgence that he might have used to a child.

"No . . . we would only run into the usual crowd and you'd hate it," she said bluntly . . . and wondered why she found it so difficult to respond to the occasional tenderness in his approach when she loved him so much.

She was always aware that he regarded her as an appealing and rather spoiled child — and she did not want to be humoured and petted and indulged. All her life she had gone her own way . . . and wished that someone cared sufficiently to check her headstrong progress. Motherless from birth, a succession of nurses and governesses had found her too wilful and too hot-tempered to handle. Her father had scarcely recognised her existence and allowed her to suppose that he could not forgive her for being the innocent cause of her mother's death in childbirth. Spenser as a schoolboy had regarded her with resentment and dislike . . . in later years he had treated her with an affectionate and tolerant indulgence that could not bridge the gap in their ages and he had always been too involved with estate affairs to have time for the problems which beset a young girl floundering on the threshold of maturity. Victoria often thought that it was no thanks to anyone but herself that she had reached womanhood without a single stain on her reputation. She had fallen in love with Luke and married him in the belief that he would provide her with the anchor that she desperately needed . . . and it hurt that he had failed her just as had everyone else.

She moved towards the door . . . and Luke watched her with faint resignation in his eyes. She gave him so little encouragement to go on loving her and yet he knew that nothing could destroy his need for the beautiful, selfish and coolly confident girl that he had married . . .

Victoria slept badly and woke with a migraine. She cancelled her engagements for the day and managed to persuade

Luke that he had no need to cancel the business appointments that would take him from the house during most of the day. It was a relief to be alone . . . Luke's kindness and solicitude were almost too much for her self-control. Yet within an hour she was longing for company. She was feeling very much better and very bored when Spenser called on her in the early afternoon. She laid aside the book that she had been half-heartedly scanning and greeted him with eager warmth.

Spenser kissed the cheek that she offered and noticed that she looked unusually pale. A telephone call to Georgina that morning had elicited the information that Victoria had cancelled a lunch appointment. He had courteously offered to take his sister's place and when he left Georgina he had decided to call on Victoria in the hope of finding her at home. She had pleaded a headache but, knowing his sister, he would not have been surprised to discover that she had extricated herself from lunching with Georgina in order to meet Marlowe.

"I'm having a lazy day," she told him lightly. "I *am* glad to see you . . . Luke has been out for hours and I hate my own company."

"Tired . . . or off colour?" he asked gently.

"A little of both," she admitted.

"Georgina told me that you'd cancelled a lunch date. I stepped into your shoes." He smiled as she flashed him a swift glance of enquiry. "Oh, I've nothing to report . . . I don't mean to rush things. I need time to stiffen my resolution, for one thing — and if I had thought of raising the subject I should have chosen very different surroundings. I may not be a romantic but I do object to proposing marriage to any woman who is more interested in the menu than her company."

Victoria chuckled. "Were you very bored?" she asked sympathetically. "Whenever I lunch with Georgina

I always wish she would enjoy the food instead of discussing its merits at length. She will pride herself on being something of a gourmet."

"The conversation was rather too culinary at times for my taste," he admitted, his eyes twinkling. "I'm inclined to think that I could endure horses rather than food as the main subject of conversation for the rest of my life." He regarded his sister thoughtfully for a moment. "What do you and Luke talk about, I wonder . . . do you bore each other, Victoria?" he asked lightly.

She shrugged. "We are very seldom alone," she said carelessly. "Bore each other? No, I don't think we do . . . not yet, anyway."

"Then that isn't your problem," he said quietly.

She stiffened. "We have no problems," she said swiftly, defensively . . . "Luke and I understand each other, Spenser."

"You have your friends and interests — and Luke remains discreetly in the background," he commented dryly. "An excellent recipe for marriage."

"It works very well," she said tautly. "Luke has his own friends, too . . . and we have several interests in common."

"He is good to you . . . kind to you?" he asked abruptly, coming to the point.

"Of course . . . more than kind," she said swiftly, defensively. "A much better husband than I deserve, no doubt . . . he never denies me anything." She smiled at her brother but it was a distinctly shaky smile and there was a suspicious brightness in the lovely eyes.

"I gave him credit for more intelligence," Spenser said dryly.

Her eyes flashed with annoyance. But she merely said airily: "Surely you don't think my marriage is on the rocks simply because Luke and I don't live in each other's pocket?"

"I don't care to hear that you are living in Julius Marlowe's pocket," he told her bluntly.

She shrugged her slim shoulders. "Oh, if you believe that stupid gossip . . . Julius is amusing and I like him, that's all. Rakes always did fascinate me. But I won't do anything stupid, Spenser . . . you may credit *me* with that much intelligence!"

"It doesn't do you any good to have your name linked with a man of Marlowe's reputation, Victoria," he warned.

Again she shrugged. "While they are tearing me to shreds they are leaving someone else alone . . . and my shoulders are broad, my dear," she said carelessly.

"Don't you care about Luke's feelings in the matter?" he countered swiftly.

A faint shadow touched her eyes . . . so swiftly was it gone that he could not be sure it had ever existed. "Are you so sure that it matters to him?" she said lightly.

Spenser frowned. "He appears to be devoted to you."

The grimness in his expression

cautioned her to say no more. "Oh, he is," she said hastily. "And he trusts me, my dear . . . I assure you that he doesn't attach any importance to my liking for Julius Marlowe. But are you really so concerned, Spenser?" she asked in surprise for it was unlike him to betray more than a casual interest in her affairs.

"The rumour that you and Luke are on the point of separating naturally concerns me," he told her dryly. "Scandal has never yet touched our name . . . I should dislike it very much if your behaviour brought it into disrepute."

She might resent his greater concern for the family name than for her happiness but understood it . . . the pride of the Chadwicks was particularly fierce in Spenser and sufficiently strong in herself to keep her out of dangerous waters in the past. She knew all the risks of friendship with Julius Marlowe but she found it difficult to resist the skilful ardour of his pursuit which was in such marked contrast to the cold acceptance and tolerance that Luke displayed. She did not mean to get out of her depth and knew that she must soon extricate herself from a flirtation that she had begun in a foolish and desperate attempt to rouse Luke to jealousy.

"People say such stupid things," she said with scorn. "There isn't any likelihood of a separation. I've no desire to leave Luke . . . and I think he's content with me for all my faults," she added lightly.

"I hoped he would encourage you to remedy a few of them," Spenser said dryly. "But he seems to be a very indulgent husband."

"Yes . . . which is something you'll never be," she retorted, neatly turning the subject. "I almost feel sorry for Georgina . . . if you really mean to marry her?"

Spenser smiled. "Who knows?" he countered.

"I wish you wouldn't," she said impulsively.

He raised a quizzical eyebrow. "Oh . . . ? Last night you approved . . . certainly you assured me that she was my best bet," he reminded her, smiling.

"So she is if you are determined to marry without love. She is as cold-blooded as you are," she declared bluntly. "She doesn't care a snap of her fingers for anyone but herself and never will. But you could be so different if only you'd allow yourself to fall in love — and there must be one woman in the world who can penetrate your armour."

Her words touched a chord of memory and he looked at her quickly. "My . . . armour?" he echoed in surprise, exactly as he had when that same criticism had been levelled at him on the previous evening.

"Your determination not to love," Victoria explained frankly. "I don't know if it's pride or reserve or the fear of exposing yourself to all the dangers of caring too much . . . or whether you've merely become so cynical that you simply can't believe that anyone could love you. It is an armour, Spenser — your protection against being hurt. I know . . . it was the same with me at one time. But it wasn't so ingrained in me . . . you see, I always wanted to be loved. I think it no longer matters to you . . . if it ever did."

He looked at her in astonishment for her tone held deep regret and their relationship had always been so casually accepted by them both that he had not thought she was so fond of him or so concerned about him. He seldom paused to wonder if he lacked anything in life . . . for the most part, he was too busy and too content.

"No, I don't think it does," he said honestly. "I'm very self-sufficient, you know."

"Nonsense!" she retorted tartly. "We all need to be loved . . . and it's natural to respond to loving."

He laughed. "Then I was born without a heart," he said carelessly.

"That's what everyone says," she said slowly. "That you are without warmth or tenderness or real interest in other people . . . that you are a cold and unemotional man with an instinctive dislike of being involved in personal relationships. But I suppose you don't care what people say about you?"

"Not in the least . . . " he drawled . . . but he was surprised to discover that he was still vulnerable enough to be vaguely hurt by the realisation of how he appeared to the world . . . a self-centred, self-satisfied man whose natural reserve indicated neither need nor desire to be liked or loved. Was he truly so self-sufficient as he believed . . . and as the world supposed? At heart he was a man like any other . . . in earlier years, he had expected to fall in love and to know the kind of happiness that other people seemed to value so much and which he found difficult even to imagine. But the passing years had brought an awareness of a certain lack in him that made it impossible for him to give so much of himself to any woman . . . and he appreciated that any woman must be repelled by the cold indifference that he scarcely attempted to conceal.

Love was beyond his understanding . . . he held the wholly cynical view that it was no more than a biological impulse designed for the propagation of the human race and that a certain reluctance in most people to face facts encouraged them to wrap an unpalatable truth in a fantasy of sentiment and romance. He was one of the very few who refused to contribute to the deceit . . . and he had very little patience with the nonsense that was uttered in the name of love.

Liking, affection, respect, trust and compassion were all emotions that he admitted to exist and he appreciated that they might easily be confused and mingled with a physical attraction so that the resultant effect persuaded people to describe themselves as being 'in love' but he could not accept that there could be a spiritual quality in that affliction. He did not object to the existence of the emotion that people called love . . . obviously it had the power of creating great happiness and equally great heartbreak. But he knew that it could never play any part in his own life.

"Why should you care?" Victoria attacked tartly. "After all, you never lack for liking and admiration . . . and you never have to exert yourself in any way to acquire these things. You give nothing and get so much in return . . . it simply isn't fair!"

"I'm just naturally irresistible," he said dryly, his eyes twinkling. "All the world loves a lord."

She moved impatiently. "It isn't that at all, Spenser . . . and I wish you weren't such a cynic. There's something about you that draws people . . . I don't know what it is but I think it's an unfortunate charm for you've never had to make the least effort to win friends.

Inevitably you take your popularity for granted . . . and I'm afraid you are becoming very arrogant," she added ruefully.

"Suddenly I am being attacked on all sides," he said in laughing reproach. "Last night a complete stranger informed me that I am so stuffed with pride that almost everyone is beneath my notice . . . and now you are accusing me of arrogance. What must I do to redeem my character?"

Victoria smiled reluctantly. "I don't know . . . I'm afraid it may be too late," she said lightly, half in earnest. "But who dared to say that to you?"

"Even if it is true?" he countered, smiling.

She was disconcerted for she had been thinking that the accusation was not wholly undeserved. She had not been blind to the cold disapproval in his appraisal of her friends the previous evening but she was too inured to his habitual dislike of most of her associates to be surprised or dismayed. She knew that his aloofness was usually assumed to stem from pride. He was proud, of course, but his natural reserve was the fairer explanation for the cool courtesy that was almost all he bestowed on most people.

"Of course it isn't true!" she refuted stoutly. "You're not a snob, Spenser!"

"Merely arrogant," he drawled pleasantly.

For all his lightness of tone, Victoria knew that he was dismayed. For it was entirely unconscious arrogance and he was a man who always respected the feelings of others although he might not share their vulnerability to hurt and humiliation.

"Never mind," she said, smiling affectionately at her brother. "Perhaps you'll grow out of it. But I thought I should mention it . . . I hope you'll dine with us tomorrow. No party, I promise — just a few people who won't bore you too much. I don't think you know them and I should be sorry if they thought you too proud to be pleasant to strangers."

"So should I!" he exclaimed involuntarily. A wry smile curved his lips. "You are giving me an excellent character, I must say. You never used to be so frank . . . is that Luke's influence?"

She laughed softly. "I don't think so . . . Sophy's perhaps," she added with an ease that implied he must know her friend.

"Sophy . . . ?" he queried politely, the name meaning nothing to him.

She raised an eyebrow. "Sophy Ransome, the general's daughter."

"I don't think I know her," he said carelessly.

She was about to argue with him, knowing that she had introduced them at her wedding and a little indignant on her friend's behalf that he should have forgotten so memorable a girl when it suddenly occurred to her that it might well have been Sophy that he had encountered on the previous night. If so, it would be amusing to bring them together and watch their reaction to each other . . . and she rather thought that the outspoken young woman who had attacked him had made a considerable impact on her brother. So she merely said carelessly: "Perhaps not. I've known her for years, of course, but she has been abroad so much that we've only become close friends in the last few months. The general is permanently settled at the War Office for the time being so we have been able to meet very often. She is dining with us tomorrow and I should like you to know her."

"I know the general. Is his daughter as swift to speak her mind . . . he has often caused a furore with that fault," Spenser commented dryly.

"Do you consider it a fault? I find it rather attractive," she returned lightly. "So many people only say what they suppose one wishes to hear. But you will come tomorrow? You will like the Raines, I know . . . and I think that Sophy will amuse you."

"Yes, I'll come . . . and for your sake I'll undertake to be wholly charming to your friends even if it is quite out of character for me," he assured her with a twinkle in his eyes. He rose to his feet. "I only called in for a few moments to see how you are . . . forgive me for dashing away but I've an appointment at three-thirty."

She smiled at him. "I wish you could stay longer . . . but I won't try to keep you. We'll see you tomorrow, then . . . Luke will be pleased. I've invited the others for seven-thirty but perhaps you will come a little earlier so we may have you to ourselves for a while?"

"So that you may advise me how to appear to the best advantage before your friends?" he mocked gently. "You are so transparent, Victoria."

"Oh, you know how to be charming without instruction from me," she retorted crisply . . . but her eyes danced with laughter at his words.

Pausing by the door, he looked at

his sister with a hint of mischief in his smile. "Shall I charm your friend into marrying me?" he asked lightly. "If you are so fond of her you might be happy to have her in the family. And it is really of little importance to me whom I marry . . . provided she is eligible and reasonably good to look at over the breakfast table."

She threw her book at him with a tolerably good aim and he dodged it, laughing. "Go away, you arrogant devil!" she exclaimed in mock irritation. "I wish Sophy was here to reply to that . . . you would soon discover if she resembles her father for blunt speaking!"

He went from the room . . . and the echo of his chuckle implied that he was not at all repentant. The smile lingered in Victoria's eyes but he had given her food for thought and she spent a very pleasant hour evolving a variety of schemes which might teach him a long-overdue lesson. But most of them would require the assistance of Sophy with her lively wit and fierce dislike of all forms of conceit and it was most unlikely that she could persuade her friend to cooperate. Sophy was not a dissembler and she would never pretend to either dislike or affection if none existed . . .

4

SPENSER strolled out to the terrace, his drink in his hand. He had arrived early as requested but Victoria had not yet left her room and Luke had been called to the telephone. It was a pleasant evening and the slanting rays of the sun fell across the pretty, well-kept gardens.

He was rapidly becoming bored and restless and now that the estate business that had brought him to town was completed he was tempted to return to Staples before the end of the week. For some reason, the sense of urgency which had prompted him to do something about his inevitable marriage was fading and he was inclined to leave matters as they were for the time being. There was no need to rush into matrimony . . . he was not yet thirty-five and in excellent health and, barring accidents, he should be able to enjoy several years of continued freedom before the need for an heir became acute.

He had found himself studying Georgina with a very critical eye . . . attractive and intelligent and very elegant though she might be, he still hesitated to ask her to be his wife. He had been so sure that he wanted no more than ordinary liking and mild affection in his wife that it came as something of a shock to discover that he resented Georgina's cool and casual response to his attentions. He wondered if he really knew what he wanted in the woman he must marry. He did not want a wife who supposed herself in love with him . . . that would make too many demands on him and possibly instil him with a sense of guilt at his inability to respond. But nor did he want a wife who regarded him with virtual indifference even though he offered little more for his part. He shrugged his broad shoulders . . . in truth, he did not want to marry at all and was seizing on the least obstacle to the success of such a cold-blooded marriage to postpone it almost indefinitely.

He knew his duty and would certainly carry it out but he need not feel that he had failed his duty if he avoided marriage for a few more years, he assured himself. His present way of life suited him very well and he would not welcome a disruption of his bachelor contentment just yet.

He set his empty glass on a small table and brought out his cigarette case. Luke's call from New York was obviously a lengthy one . . . and he knew from experience that Victoria would not descend until the last moment. He had no wish to introduce himself to his sister's friends who were due that evening . . . he decided to remain on the terrace and enjoy a quiet cigarette.

Leaning against the stone balustrade, absently watching a bird who had perched on the edge of the small fountain to trill his evensong, his thoughts turned inevitably to his home in the heart of the country . . . and he was startled out of his reverie by a low and rather attractive voice that wished him good evening with quiet self-possession. He turned swiftly, staring at the girl who was framed in the open window and then a slow smile dawned in his eyes. He bowed slightly. "Miss Ransome . . . the general's daughter, I believe," he murmured.

Amusement leaped to her eyes. "Sounds rather like Happy Families . . . but I'm flattered that you have recalled my name," she said lightly, mockingly.

His smile deepened. "I am indebted to my sister for the information. I cannot tell a lie, you see."

"It does you credit," she assured him serenely.

"Not at all . . . I knew you would not believe me if I declared that your name had only temporarily slipped my mind," he retorted dryly.

"You never knew it, of course."

"I don't think I did," he agreed frankly.

"And you still cannot remember where we met," she said lightly . . . and it was not a question.

"No."

She shook her head at him in reproach but her eyes were dancing . . . and the roguish mischief in those green, long-lashed eyes completely dispelled his impression that she was no beauty. Perhaps she was not beautiful in the accepted sense of the word . . . her chin a little too pointed, her mouth a little too wide for beauty, something of the gamin in the wicked demurity of her expression — but she possessed an appeal that was entirely her own.

"I won't bore you with the details but it was some months ago," she told him carelessly.

"Victoria's wedding!" he exclaimed.

She nodded. "How could you be expected to remember everyone you met on that occasion?" she asked demurely.

"We danced together," he suddenly recalled.

"We did . . . and exchanged at least two sentences that were not at all memorable," she said, smiling.

"I must have been very dull company."

"Oh, you were," she agreed lightly. "But I appreciated the compliment . . . it quite made my evening a success. Such marked interest . . . the talk of the town for days, I assure you!"

Spenser laughed. "You really are your father's daughter, aren't you? Every remark uttered with malice aforethought! It makes it rather difficult for me to decide if you merit my attention, you know," he said lightly, mockingly.

"Oh . . . ? I don't have that problem," she told him carelessly. "I disliked you on sight and I see no reason to change my mind."

Spenser was taken aback by the blunt words, spoken so coolly. He could not doubt that her dislike was genuine . . . this girl was wholly indifferent to his opinion of her and therefore felt no need to utter the conventional pleasantries.

"You are certainly an original," he commented dryly.

"Please don't feel that you must pay me compliments," she said sweetly. "Ordinary courtesy will be quite acceptable . . . if you won't find that too difficult?"

Spenser scarcely knew whether to be amused or infuriated . . . at least he should not be bored, he thought wryly. The evening would hold a degree of interest in wondering what next this odd, outspoken girl would say or do to dispel his first instinctive liking.

"You must forgive me if the lurking beast slips its leash occasionally," he said dryly. "I suspect you are likely to provoke it from time to time." He studied her coolly. "Victoria has been quite taken in," he went on pleasantly. "She spoke of you so warmly that it's disconcerting to discover that her dearest Sophy is the very person who admitted me to the intimate circle of her *bête noires* at first sight."

"I've heard you discussed in glowing terms, too," she returned lightly. "So amazing . . . !"

Victoria appeared at the open widow in time to hear the exchange with all its undercurrents and brief consternation touched her lovely face. She had so wanted them to like each other, she thought ruefully . . . but it was just what she should have expected after indulging the foolish hope that Sophy might be the one woman to bring out all the latent warmth and tenderness in Spenser's nature. Concealing her chagrin, she announced her presence by declaring gaily: "As a hostess I'm a miserable failure! I'm so sorry, Sophy . . . has Spenser been looking after you? I gather that you've introduced yourselves . . . "

"We had already met," Spenser enlightened her.

"Oh . . . that's wonderful!" Victoria declared happily, choosing to ignore the coolness of the atmosphere. She beamed on them with impartial delight. "Now the evening *will* be a success," she said with naive optimism.

Instinctively Spenser and Sophy glanced at each other in wry amusement . . . and Victoria's hopes were instantly revived. If they shared a sense of humour it was something, she thought confidently . . . and did not mind that she was the cause of their mutual amusement. Perhaps she had sounded insouciant but it was so much more comfortable to pretend that all was well even when it was blatantly not well at all . . . and it was better that they should dislike each other than regard each other with indifference, after all.

They followed her into the house as she said lightly: "I'm afraid things have been badly mismanaged. I was late coming down and assumed that Luke was looking after you. But I gather he's tied up with a call from New York. I'm so sorry, Sophy . . . "

"It really doesn't matter," Sophy

assured her lightly. She accepted the offer of a drink but shook her head to a cigarette and Spenser sank into an armchair and listened idly to the conversation between the two women while they waited for Luke and the other members of the party. He had ample opportunity to observe the extent of his sister's affection for her friend . . . and he studied Sophy Ransome with faint curiosity, endeavouring to discover what it was about the girl that had charmed Victoria so completely.

He was soon to discover that she was equally popular with everyone and yet she did not possess an obvious charm nor did she seem to seek the attentions that came her way throughout the evening and which were received with a faint air of deprecation. Victoria was a very lovely young woman with her copper-coloured hair, her slender height, her vivacity and elegance — but she did not overshadow the rather plain girl in the simply cut gown. Spenser liked the quiet bearing and the gentle dignity which sat a little oddly on such young shoulders yet was decidedly attractive. He knew that comparisons were odious but he could not help noticing how quiet and unaffected and level-headed she seemed in contrast to Victoria's bubbling high spirits and rather flippant attitudes. She could be very little older than Victoria but she possessed a maturity and a self-possession that struck him as unusual for her years.

Seated beside him, she treated him with an ease of manner that ignored her antipathy without actually concealing it from him. He was tempted to applaud her skill but there was just a hint of amused provocation in her attitude that he resolutely refused to answer by word or manner. She was a minx, he thought, faintly amused — and he chose to respond with cool, pleasant courtesy. He knew exactly how little importance to attach to her conventional interest and attention — and set out to bestow much of his considerable charm on the other members of that dinner-party. He knew that Victoria was just a little anxious for the success of the evening but failed to convince himself that his readiness to be pleased by the Raines was entirely for his sister's benefit. He knew very well that Sophy Ransome could not fail to appreciate her subtle exclusion from his warm friendliness and disarming attentions. It was not obviously done, of course . . . he would not care to expose anyone to the inevitable comment that must follow any marked neglect on his part. But Sophy could not be in any doubt that his enjoyment of the evening owed nothing to her presence . . . and that was exactly what he wished to convey to her.

He was still smarting from her attack — and his reaction to the realisation that a virtual stranger had judged him and found him wanting caused him to wonder ruefully if he had indeed become so arrogant. It had always irritated him that people were so ready to like and admire him, so eager for his friendship, so impressed by his rank and wealth and social standing. But it was oddly more irritating to meet a chit of a girl who did not even pretend to like him and was not at all impressed by anything about him. He could not deny that he resented her hasty judgement or that his first amused astonishment had been replaced by a vague sense of injury.

He did not dislike her . . . he was neither hasty nor impulsive and he scarcely knew Sophy Ransome. He was a little intrigued by the quiet, deceptively demure young woman with the alarming candour and quaint dignity — but mild interest was not liking. Perhaps he would not have given her a second thought if she had not treated him to the rough edge of her tongue but he did not suspect her of using that method to attract him. Without conceit, he felt that she did not whole-heartedly dislike him for all the display of antagonism . . . she might despise certain facets of his personality which had become exaggerated through circumstances but the hint of laughter in her clear green eyes whenever she turned or spoke to him convinced him that she was enjoying the thrust and parry of their verbal encounters. So was he, he realised with faint surprise . . . there was an attractive novelty in the situation and for the first time in years he did not feel the boredom which so often affected his enjoyment of any social occasion . . .

Spenser was not attracted but he found himself liking the girl almost against his will as the evening progressed. She was a very warm person, he decided, noting the sincerity of her smile when it was not meant for himself, the sweetness of her expression in repose, the genuine interest she brought to the most trivial of conversations, the subtle courtesy and consideration in the way she distributed her attention. He thought wryly that she bore all the hallmarks of the experienced hostess — and he wished that Victoria were not quite so careless of her rôle. It did not seem to occur to his thoughtless sister that it was her duty to ensure the enjoyment and entertainment of her guests . . . having brought together a handful of people, she adopted the attitude that she had played her part in creating a successful dinner-party. Without taking over her friend's rôle, Sophy nevertheless introduced just the right note of warm and easy intimacy into the evening and contrived to bring out the best in everyone with consummate skill.

The reserved Paul Raines blossomed into an amusing and very skilled raconteur who held them all enthralled as they sat around the blazing log fire with coffee and liqueurs and cigarettes. Luke, a brilliant pianist who combined a love of music with intuitive understanding of its interpretation, was persuaded to play although it was seldom that he did so in public. Anna Raines, an artist whose work had recently been acclaimed by the critics, was encouraged to talk more freely about her work than Spenser had achieved for all his earlier efforts. Her extensive experience of other countries together with a gift for describing odd and amusing incidents with a flair that brought them vividly to life held everyone's interest.

When the conversation turned to general subjects, skimming lightly over plays and films and books, celebrities of stage and screen, the latest fashions in clothes and manners, Spenser found that Sophy's gaze rested on him with a hint of speculation in their green depths. He strolled to her side on the pretext of offering his cigarette case and, as she bent her head over the flame of his lighter, he murmured softly, mockingly: "I am not grist for your mill, my girl . . . you must do without my contribution."

She looked up at him with that deceptively sweet smile he already anticipated and mistrusted. "I suppose so," she said regretfully. "The life of a country squire however well described, must certainly compare badly with our cosmopolitan junketings."

His eyes narrowed at the unmistakable implication that his preference for country rather than town life and his dislike of the social round made him virtually a dead loss as a conversationalist. "Very likely," he retorted, a trifle grimly. "It would be difficult to explain its appeal to you, of course."

"Oh no . . . surely not?" she countered with a grave innocence that belied the laughter in her eyes. "The attraction is obvious . . . after all, at Staples you are master and may be as proud as you please without risk of criticism."

His eyes sparked with sudden anger . . . he turned away abruptly and distinctly heard the soft and very provocative little chuckle that escaped her lips. He swung on his heel but she met his furious eyes with such an innocent enquiry in her own that he could not help smiling although he itched to wring her slender neck. "Your round, I think," he conceded dryly — and was rewarded by a swift and genuinely warm smile that touched her rather plain face to sudden beauty.

Provocative little wretch, he thought grimly — and wondered if she could possibly be justified in considering him more of a liability than an asset to any social function. Was he really such a dull dog, he wondered ruefully. He seldom exerted himself to contribute to the success of any affair as he had done that evening . . . and with much less success than Sophy Ransome who had not even appeared to be trying, he thought wryly.

He was by nature a quiet and reticent man and his dislike of social affairs stemmed from the ingrained boredom and cynical distaste that was due to being the focus of too much attention on too many occasions for too many years. He had enjoyed this particular evening, however, taking a lively interest in his companions, and he would be sorry to see it come to an end — but he realised that for the most part he had been a silent listener, expecting to be entertained without exerting himself unduly to entertain. It would not be surprising if he had given the impression that he was bored and indifferent and 'too proud to be pleased', as Victoria had described his manner with such surprising bluntness.

He was not usually given to self-analysis, having little time or inclination for the luxury, and it was disconcerting that a mere chit of a girl whom he did not even like could prompt him to search his soul in the attempt to discover if he could be as shallow and contemptible as she appeared to think him. He had never supposed himself to be the fine fellow that everyone assured him that he was but he realised with a faint shock that he had certainly acquired a degree of unconscious arrogance if he was so irritated by the criticism of a virtual stranger . . .

It was almost midnight when the

party began to break up . . . Victoria, discovering that Sophy's car was temporarily in dock, had no hesitation in offering her brother's services as an escort. Spenser had no choice but to second the offer with as good a grace as he could muster.

Sophy preferred to be independent but she noticed the fleeting annoyance in Spenser Chadwick's expression and immediately thanked him with demurity in her voice and laughter lurking in her eyes. She knew that she had been a thorn in his side all the evening . . . she was not at all surprised that he did not welcome the thought of taking her home.

She had been mischievously delighted by his slightly-pointed attentions to their fellow-guests and she had been thankful for it, preferring an amused and disinterested courtesy to the marked attentions which would have convinced her that he was as conceited as she had supposed him to be from their first encounter.

Courteously he handed her into his car and closed the door on her before making his way round to the driving seat . . . but there was an austerity in his manner that betrayed his irritation with Victoria's generosity on his behalf. He set the car in motion in silence . . . and a little gurgle of involuntary amusement broke from her lips.

Spenser glanced at her briefly. "I seem to afford you a great deal of amusement in one way and another," he commented.

"You are such a reluctant cavalier!" she explained, her eyes dancing.

A faint smile touched his lips. "You are mistaken," he drawled. "I merely dislike being pressed into service by my sister. How can I claim any credit for a generous gesture when you are not likely to believe that it was in my mind before Victoria spoke?"

"I might believe it if I had cause to suppose that generous gestures were a habit with you," she said serenely.

"You have no cause to suppose

otherwise," he pointed out caustically.

"Call it feminine intuition," she retorted lightly.

Spenser laughed reluctantly. "You have all the makings of a shrew, my girl," he said bluntly but the amused appreciation in his eyes took the sting from the words.

Sophy smiled absently. She was not really at a loss for an answer . . . merely shaken by the realisation that her heart had given an odd little leap as their eyes met. How very strange when she did not consider him at all attractive, she thought dispassionately . . .

"Perhaps my tongue is a little impulsive," she admitted without regret.

"Oh, no need to apologise," he said, a little dryly. "I value the good opinion of my friends but the rest of the world may think what they choose about me, you know."

"How fortunate that all the world thinks well of a lord," she replied sweetly . . . but she was vaguely hurt by the words that excluded her so pointedly from his friendship. She could scarcely expect anything else when she had deliberately sought to alienate him, she thought fairly — and wondered why she should feel that his friendship could be valuable. He was not a man that inspired her to liking or admiration, after all.

Spenser made no reply and there was a faint grimness about his expression that puzzled Sophy. He was obviously annoyed and she wondered which of her many thrusts had found a target . . . and why. Her original antagonism towards him had evaporated in the enjoyment of their duel of wits and it had not occurred to her that anything she might say could really wound him. But the sudden and ominous silence made her wonder if he was more vulnerable to criticism and harsh comment than she had supposed.

Reviewing the evening, she conceded that he had a great deal of charm when he chose to exert it. He was certainly an attractive man with his striking good looks, powerful physique and impressive air . . . it was not surprising that so many women were disposed to like him, to court his friendship and welcome his attentions. The streak of perversity in her make-up had been fired by the extravagant descriptions applied to him by other women and she had made up her mind to dislike Spenser Chadwick long before that first meeting. She had been forced to concede that he was quite as attractive and personable as everyone claimed — but she had immediately detected the fault that most people obviously chose to overlook. He was arrogant beyond bearing.

She had dismissed him from her mind until his unexpected arrival at Victoria's party when she had viewed him with renewed dislike and contempt as she noticed his reluctance to be drawn into conversation by people who did not interest him. Preceding him to the terrace by only a few moments, she had foolishly supposed that he had followed her to renew their acquaintance. His glance had passed over her as though she did not exist . . . and her reaction to that indifference had been all the more forceful because she had been surprised into smiling a warm greeting. Anxious to rid his mind of any misapprehension, she had whipped her resentment to anger — and when he turned, sensing her hostility, she had taken the opportunity to cross swords with him.

In retrospect, the encounter had been amusing . . . and she admitted that he had answered her with surprising good humour and seemed almost likeable during those few moments when his amusement had overcome indignation.

She had not expected to see him again so soon. Wandering to the open window while she waited for Luke or Victoria to make an appearance, she had been briefly disconcerted to recognise the proud head with the unusual blaze of white in the rich copper. She had known a fleeting and strange sensation of pleasure that she had swiftly construed as anticipation of the enjoyment she would find in baiting him throughout the evening. And she had enjoyed it, she thought . . . it had delighted her to know that at moments he had been almost goaded to sharp and scathing retort.

Her first active dislike for him now seemed a little foolish and unjust . . . a hasty, emotional judgement. She had no real reason to dislike and despise him — it was merely that her vanity had been piqued by his proud indifference. She still thought him arrogant but that might be forgivable in a man who had been showered with fawning and flattering attentions for so many years. There was no harm in liking him, of course — but there might be danger in seeing too much of a man who was decidedly and disturbingly attractive, she thought warily.

5

AS the car drew into the forecourt of the block of luxury apartments where she lived with her father, Sophy turned to her still-silent companion with a friendly smile. "Thank you so much for bringing me home. You'll come in for a drink, won't you? My father will be delighted to give you a nightcap and I believe you already know each other?"

On the point of refusing, Spenser changed his mind. His annoyance was abruptly dispelled by the smile that warmed her eyes and brought a certain sweetness to her face. It was a wholly enchanting smile without any of the mischievous, self-possessed mockery that he already associated with this unusual young woman. He was puzzled by that warm friendliness . . . he could not believe that she liked him at all and yet she smiled as warmly as though they had never been anything but friends.

Following her into the entrance hall and towards the waiting lift, he decided that she was entirely lacking in coquetry. She seemed to have a natural sweetness and warm generosity of disposition for all the wicked humour and mischievous malice of a quick tongue.

The General was a gregarious man and he greeted Spenser with warm cordiality, insisted on giving him a drink and a cigar and monopolised his attention to the extent that Sophy was virtually forgotten. Curled in an armchair, she fought a sudden sleepiness and listened to Spenser's courteous interest in her father's diatribe against the latest follies of a government he had never supported. She was a little surprised by Spenser's intelligent grasp of the political situation both at home and overseas . . . she had foolishly supposed that he took little interest in anything but his land and his personal affairs.

It was some time before the General left them with an embarrassing display of tact. Sophy, aware that her cheeks were burning, found Spenser regarding her with amusement and she was briefly disconcerted.

She rose from her armchair and moved towards the decanters.

"Another drink . . . ?"

He shook his head. "No . . . I'm driving," he reminded her with a faint smile. "I must go, Sophy."

It was the first time he had used her name and her heart gave an odd little jump. She was surprised to discover how pretty her name could sound on a man's lips . . . and the easy friendliness of his tone was very disarming.

He raised a quizzical eyebrow. "What is it?"

She realised that she was staring at him in faint dismay. Quickly she pulled herself together. "Nothing . . . nothing at all," she returned lightly, coolly.

He smiled. "You looked at me as

though you had never really seen me before," he told her dryly.

"Did I? But I wasn't even thinking about you," she assured him carelessly. She was suddenly wary . . . he was so tall, so handsome, so vibrantly masculine, filling the room with his magnetism and evoking a strange and bewildering excitement in her blood. It would never do to betray that swift reaction to the physical magnetism of this man . . . and she was wise enough to know that physical attraction was never to be trusted. He was really much too attractive, she thought wryly. She held out her hand to him. "Thank you again for bringing me home."

Spenser sensed the dismissal in her tone — and perversely he did not choose to be dismissed although only a moment before he had been anxious to be on his way. But he took the proffered hand . . . such a small delicate hand, he thought unexpectedly. Tenderness stirred, surprising him, as those slender fingers fluttered briefly in the warm imprisonment of his clasp. He looked down into the clear green eyes that met his own so steadily and said slowly, deliberately: "You and I could be friends, Sophy." A rare impulse had provoked the words but immediately they were uttered he knew it had been a mistake.

Sophy was shaken. The sudden warmth in his eyes was unexpected and she scarcely knew how to interpret it. Was he aware of her response to his physical attractions . . . was this a preliminary to light flirtation?

She sent him a quizzical glance and said lightly: "Then I should lose the pleasure of fencing with you. One has to curb one's tongue too much where friends are concerned and I enjoy our encounters too much to want your friendship, I'm afraid."

Spenser laughed and knew a swift gratitude that she had not taken him up on those impulsive words, born of a momentary emotion that he could not really analyse. She was an intriguing young woman but he did not want to become too involved with her . . . it was much wiser to keep their relationship on its present footing. "I might find it difficult to remember that we are not on friendly terms," he told her, smiling.

"Oh, I shall remind you," she assured him airily, her eyes twinkling.

When he had gone, Sophy went to bed — but not immediately to sleep. Curled up on her side with a hand cradling her cheek, she stared into the darkness seeing very clearly the handsome face and mocking eyes and proud auburn head of Spenser Chadwick. She was dismayed by the discovery that it would be very easy for her to tumble into love with the man she had been so ready to despise. In that moment when he had clasped her hand and looked steadily into her eyes, her heart had lurched suddenly and painfully. She thanked heaven for the instinct which had helped her over a dangerous moment by urging her to return a light and mocking answer to his words. She knew only too well that friendship with this particular man would very soon cease to satisfy her . . . she also realised that it would be folly to hope for anything more. She had no real reason to quarrel with the general opinion that he was cold, proud and self-sufficient, a man who would not give his heart easily if at all.

She wondered when she would see him again — and told herself that she had no desire to see him again. She must put him out of her mind and forget this ridiculous fancy that he was the only man who could inspire her to loving. Of all the men in the world it was quite absurd to suppose that she could care for Spenser Chadwick with his contemptible arrogance and deplorable cynicism and soul-destroying indifference to the thoughts and feelings of everyone but himself . . . and there could be no future in loving such a man.

He would not be in town very long, of course. She might not run into him again during his short stay but if they did chance to meet then she meant to guard her heart well by keeping him at a safe distance. Certainly it would never do to let him know by word or smile or gesture that he was responsible for this strange upheaval of her emotions. Being quite as proud as any Chadwick, Sophy was determined not to wear her heart on a sleeve or to make the mistake of yearning for something she was never likely to possess . . . and on that excellent resolution she drifted into sleep . . .

Victoria was on the telephone early the next morning, anxious to know the result of her rather obvious attempt to force a tête-à-tête on her brother and her friend. Fancying a certain coolness in Sophy's response, she said lightly: "Am I in your bad books?"

"Well, you aren't one of my favourite people just now," Sophy returned with a laugh in her voice. "How could you thrust me into your brother's arms like that!"

Victoria chuckled. "I didn't see why he shouldn't enjoy being useful for once. He was furious with me, though, wasn't he? Was I so very blatant?"

"Abominably so! You left the poor man no choice . . . but he assured me that he was merely annoyed because you forestalled him."

"Oh . . . ?"

Sophy laughed. "I don't care for that optimistic note in your voice. You are mistaken if you suppose that your brother is interested in me. . or I in him, for that matter. But this is an early call for you . . . prompted by curiosity or conscience, I wonder?"

"Now you know that I've never been troubled by a conscience," Victoria retorted gaily. "I thought we might lunch together . . . unless you have other plans?"

"Spenser didn't betray the slightest desire to meet me again if that is what is on your mind," Sophy retorted smoothly.

"How strange . . . I rather thought

he liked you and you seemed to get on so well together last night . . . "

Sophy raised an astonished eyebrow at the words. "Did you really think so?" she asked, a note of amused incredulity in her voice. "I'm afraid you're an incurable optimist, Victoria. You must ask Luke for his impressions of the evening . . . I believe he will tell you that your brother and I were at daggers drawn most of the time."

"Well, I didn't notice it," Victoria refuted stoutly and her tone implied the impossibility of such a thing.

"How should you when you were so determined to ignore our mutual antipathy?" Sophy countered lightly.

"Don't you like Spenser at all?" Victoria asked in very youthful and rather comic dismay.

Sophy laughed softly. "Must I like him?"

"Well, it would be nice," Victoria said, a little wistfully. "I'd much rather have you for a sister-in-law than that odious Georgina Winslow."

Sophy's heart stopped for a moment at the unexpected words. She was thankful that her friend was at the other end of a telephone line and unable to see the reaction to her careless remark. She managed to force a casual interest into her tone. "I wasn't aware of an engagement. But they are well-suited to each other, don't you think?"

"Perhaps I shouldn't have mentioned it . . . after all, nothing is settled. Spenser may change his mind or Georgina might not choose to marry him," Victoria said on a hopeful note. "It all seems very cold-blooded to me. I appreciate that Spenser must marry but I don't know why it has to be Georgina Winslow!"

"Every man to his taste," Sophy returned with a lightness she did not wholly feel. "I've just looked at my book, Victoria . . . I can't lunch today, I'm afraid. But you and Luke are dining here on Friday, aren't you . . . you must tell me all about it then."

Victoria replaced the receiver a little

despondently. Perhaps she had been too optimistic, too ready to believe that something could flare into life between Spenser and Sophy Ransome if only she provided a timely helping hand. But she had been encouraged by a certain glow in her brother's eyes whenever he turned to Sophy, being too blind to the provocation in her friend's manner to realise that it was a dangerous glitter rather than the glow of admiration. She had recognised the light, easy and wholly unself-conscious friendliness with which Sophy reacted to all men and she had dismissed the memory of those earlier words between them, quite unable to believe that anyone could dislike a man with so much charm and character as her brother.

In the last few months, Victoria had come to know Sophy very well and it surprised her that there was no man of real importance in her friend's life. For she seemed to inspire liking and admiration very easily, never lacking for friends, and she possessed an appeal that went beyond ordinary physical beauty. It was unthinkable that no man had ever loved Sophy but although she was generous with her affection and her loyalty she never showed the least inclination to give her heart to any man. She did not make a habit of falling in love and out again with the regularity that Victoria had come to expect in most of her girl friends. It seemed that Sophy was as hard to please as Spenser, she thought ruefully . . . and realised how much she had hoped that they would be drawn to each other. She had been so sure that even Spenser could not resist the lovable qualities that everyone else found in Sophy . . . and it would have been a great delight to watch the slow unfolding of a real and lasting romance.

But one could not manoeuvre people to suit one's own dreams, unfortunately — and Victoria had a rather pressing problem where her own affairs were concerned. Julius was becoming more demanding — and Luke continued to seem as indifferent as ever to her friendship with another man. They were drifting further and further apart with each day that passed and she was beginning to wonder if she could go on with this empty shell of a marriage . . .

Sophy sat very still for some moments after ending that telephone conversation with her friend, staring blankly at the receiver that remained in her hand.

She had been foolishly stunned by the news that Spenser Chadwick meant to marry Georgina Winslow. But it was not really so surprising, she told herself sternly . . . indeed, it was very natural that he should wish to marry a woman he had known for so long and who probably meant a great deal to him. Certainly she did not know him well enough to judge if it was a wise choice on his part but she could not help feeling that they would freeze each other to death. He seemed to be a cold and reserved man — and Georgina was notably an iceberg among women. Sophy was convinced that Spenser only needed the warmth and generosity of a loving woman to become an ardent and tender and very human lover. But she was prejudiced, of course . . . and inclining towards an abominable conceit if she could suppose that she was just the kind of woman that Spenser Chadwick needed for his happiness.

She scarcely knew him, after all. She was far from being in love with him. She was merely foolishly piqued by the discovery that he was going to be married . . . as if it could really matter to her! He was never likely to want to marry her, she told herself scornfully . . . and he was the last man in the world she could ever want for a husband, she added with an astonishing disregard for truth.

When he married Georgina Winslow she would wish him happy and forget all about him . . . and time would prove that it was a much easier thing to do than her stubborn and very silly heart insisted.

She resolved not to think any more about him — and spent the better part of a week in reminding herself of that resolve. She comforted herself again with the thought that he would soon be leaving London and they need not meet again. She admitted that the only protection for her foolish and wayward heart was not to see him again for a time . . . and at the same time she was ridiculously disappointed that their paths did not happen to cross . . .

She was busy with preparations for the party that was being given on Friday in honour of her birthday. It was not a very important birthday — her twenty-fourth — and she had resisted her father's suggestion of a big celebration, preferring a small and intimate dinner-party with just a few friends. Years of presiding as hostess for her father had taught her all the arts of entertaining and it was something she enjoyed.

She schooled herself carefully to appear unaffected by the mention of Spenser's name for it was inevitable that Victoria at least would bring him into the conversation at some time during the evening. But she was not prepared to meet him in person and her reaction was one of delight mingled with dismay when Victoria arrived with her brother as her escort.

Spenser recognised only the dismay and saw none of the delight. He glanced down at his sister and mistrusted the innocence of her expression. Sophy had been delayed by another guest on her way to welcome them and he had a moment to challenge Victoria. "Did you tell Sophy that I was taking Luke's place?" he demanded.

Victoria smiled sweetly. "It must have slipped my mind," she said carelessly. "Does it matter?"

"I don't think she is very pleased about it," he told her grimly.

"Oh, nonsense . . . I expect she's just wondering why Luke isn't with me. She is very fond of Luke, you know — they are great friends."

Sophy had recovered her composure by the time she moved forward to greet them . . . and she was quite determined to conceal how much it meant to her to have Spenser's presence at her birthday dinner. No doubt it was very foolish but this was a special day in a way and there had been a bleakness about her heart ever since she woke that morning to the realisation that she was not likely to see or speak to the one person who would make the day complete. There had been a stack of cards and telegrams but no word from Spenser Chadwick . . . flowers and gifts had arrived in a steady stream but there had been nothing from Spenser Chadwick. Of course she had appreciated that he probably did not know it was her birthday . . . but she had still been disappointed.

Her smile for Victoria was warm and

the fleeting kiss she bestowed on her friend's cheek was sincere. "How nice you look!" she said warmly. "But where is Luke?"

"He sent his love and his regrets. An urgent call came through from New York last night and he had to fly over to settle some dispute. He left on an early flight this morning . . . too early to ring you," Victoria explained. "I've brought Spenser to compensate for his absence."

"A poor substitute, I'm afraid," he commented lightly as she turned to him. "But not entirely unacceptable, I trust."

Sophy smiled — but the smile did not quite reach her eyes. "Not at all . . . I'm glad you were free to come. No hostess likes to have uneven numbers at her table, after all."

He sent her a quizzical glance. "A very gracious welcome . . . thank you!"

Her eyes began to dance. "I thought you had left town or I should certainly have sent you an invitation."

"Another disappointment?" he suggested softly.

She laughed but did not reply. She turned back to his sister. "I think you know everyone, Victoria . . . Henry is in charge of the drinks and will look after you." As another guest arrived close on their heels she left them with a murmured excuse . . . and Victoria looked after her with smiling admiration.

"I've never seen Sophy look so attractive," she declared sincerely. "I wonder where she bought that dress . . . it's superb and just right for her."

Spenser scarcely heard. But he was silently commending Sophy's appearance on this occasion. Her dress was long and flowing and very elegant, in a soft, misty grey, high at the throat, long-sleeved and almost Quakerish in its simplicity. Her hair was banded smoothly about her small, shapely head and she wore very little make-up and no jewellery. Her eyes were sparkling and her skin was glowing with health and

vitality and enjoyment of the evening
. . . and she looked more lovely than
he had supposed possible.

She did not seem the same girl who
had curled in an armchair while he
discussed politics with her father, her
eyes full of drowsy dreams . . . or the
girl who had allowed her fingers to
curve so responsively to his and looked
up at him with a sweetness of expression
that had stirred him strangely. She was
serenely self-possessed and very much
in her element, he thought . . . and
decided again that here was a born
hostess and a woman of character and
dignity and quiet charm. She was a
woman who compelled his interest
. . . and perhaps more than ordinary
interest, he thought in faint surprise.

As though she sensed his gaze, she
looked up and directly at him. Their
eyes met and held for a moment. Then
she smiled absently and returned her
attention to her companion. And in that
moment Spenser Chadwick discovered
that he had been mistaken in supposing

he would welcome indifference rather than eagerness in a woman . . .

Victoria had swiftly deserted her silent brother for more congenial company. Spenser acquired a drink and took it to a quiet corner of the room where he sat alone and content, watching his hostess as she circulated among her guests.

At last she looked for him . . . and then came towards him, smiling. But there was a coolness about that smile and something in her eyes that set him carefully at a distance. She was merely doing her duty by him, he thought dryly.

"Poor Spenser . . . are you very bored?" she asked lightly, sitting beside him on the sofa with an air of impermanency. "Victoria shouldn't have dragged you to such a dull affair."

"Do you really want me to agree with you?" he countered mockingly.

She laughed softly. "Oh, you may be as rude as you wish . . . I'm sure you are justified," she assured him. "What on earth possessed Victoria . . . she must know that this kind of party is not at all to your taste."

He smiled. "You are mistaken . . . and I'd rather she pressed me into service than chose Julius Marlowe for her escort."

"Well, she won't meet him here . . . I don't like the man," she said bluntly. She hesitated a moment and then went on: "Are you worried about Victoria? I'm sure you need not be."

"I wish I shared your confidence but it seems to me that Victoria sees far too much of a man whose reputation is deplorable."

"She is a little indiscreet," Sophy agreed reluctantly. "But I'm sure it's merely a harmless flirtation . . . she is flirting now, after all, scarcely knowing that she does it," she added with an affectionate and indulgent glance for her friend.

"Does she confide in you at all?" he asked, a little abruptly.

"Not very often . . . why do you ask?"

"You seem to be close friends. I think there is something very wrong between Victoria and Luke but I am the last person she would confide in."

She was pleased that there was a certain amount of regret in his tone . . . Victoria had given her the impression that her brother took little or no interest in her affairs.

"She doesn't talk about it to me . . . but she is very proud, you know."

"Yes, I do know," he said ruefully. "It's a family trait." A faint frown touched his eyes. "I think you are fairly perceptive, Sophy . . . I imagine you know what is wrong but you don't mean to tell me, do you?"

She met his eyes steadily. "Why not? I don't know as much as you suppose but I believe that family trait is to blame. They are both too proud to admit that anything is wrong."

"I knew he would have trouble with her," Spenser said wryly. "Luke is weak and much too dependent on other people for his happiness. She should never have married him, of course."

"I imagine that she was in love with him!" The retort was involuntary and she coloured faintly as she met the glimmer of amusement in his glance.

"All the more reason to steer clear of marriage, in my opinion . . . it's the cure for love, after all," he said lightly.

"You are a cynic, I'm afraid," she returned with some heat.

"A man doesn't get to my age without becoming cynical. When I marry it certainly won't be for love," he said firmly.

"Then why marry at all?" she demanded bluntly.

"I must, unfortunately . . . I have a duty to my name and my estates."

She said demurely: "How very inconvenient for you! I hope your wife will be obliging enough to present you with a son . . . imagine your feelings if your sacrifice was rewarded with mere daughters! But I suppose you would simply obtain a divorce and try again in those circumstances."

"Chadwicks do not indulge in the luxury of divorce," he told her with deliberate arrogance, enjoying the militant sparkle in her green eyes.

"The family trait, I suppose? How odd that it should be so active in some respects and so dormant where a marriage of convenience is concerned," she said sweetly. "Now, I'm not cursed with pride but nothing would persuade me into such a marriage . . . I value my self-respect too much!"

"Interpretation: you are a romantic gambler who would risk the happiness of a lifetime with a man you scarcely know and imagine that you love," he returned dryly. "Whereas I mean to marry a woman I know really well — and our marriage won't be complicated by the hotch-potch of fanciful notions that people so foolishly describe as 'love'." He looked at her with a malicious twinkle in his eyes. "Victoria is doing her best to bring us together, I suspect — but I promise not to offend your romantic nature with the offer of a marriage of convenience. My countess will need a much stricter rein on her tongue than you possess — and the taming of a shrew would be above and beyond the call of duty, don't you think?"

Sophy rose abruptly, her chest heaving with indignation . . . or was it laughter, he wondered suddenly. He caught her wrist in firm but gentle fingers and she turned to look at him. He found, as he had suspected, that her eyes were brimming with merriment.

"Abominable creature!" she threw at him lightly. "Let me go . . . I am neglecting *my* duty as a hostess."

He laughed softly and released her wrist. As she walked away, he looked after her and he was almost tempted to test the sincerity of her claim. There was a certain piquancy in knowing that she had not the slightest interest in marrying him . . . and he wondered

if he might not enjoy persuading her
into a change of heart even if he could
never commit himself to the folly and
the empty promise of loving her or any
other woman . . .

6

SOPHY had arranged the table plan very carefully, placing Luke on one side of her and the elderly Colonel Nesbit, her father's friend and her own godfather, on the other.

As it was too late to alter the plan, she found herself sitting next to Spenser Chadwick . . . and scarcely knew whether to be pleased or dismayed. For he virtually ignored his other dinner partner and set out to devote almost his entire attention to her. The colonel was very deaf and it was always difficult to maintain a satisfactory conversation with him so, unless she sat silent, she was compelled to talk to Spenser much more than she could have wished.

She was not encouraging. Indeed, she returned so many monosyllables to his attempts at conversation that he finally said ruefully: "I suspect that you prefer your dinner to my conversation."

She chuckled. "I suspect you are right," she said lightly. "But you must admit that we have a really excellent cook."

"And my poor efforts to entertain you cannot compete with her mastery of the culinary arts . . . I see," he said dryly.

"Oh, I find you very amusing," she assured him, smiling. "But it isn't kind of you to neglect Lady Nesbit . . . do talk to her, Spenser."

"No, no . . . don't cast me into that pit," he said quickly. "She doesn't approve of me, you know. We never meet but she tells me what an excellent man my father was and what a pity it is that men aren't cast in his mould any more. She really is a terrifying old lady."

Sophy gave a gurgle of laughter. "You are between two fires, I'm afraid," she told him lightly. "For I don't approve of you either."

"But I'm the most upright of men,"

he protested in mock indignation.

"A little too upright for my taste," she retorted, her eyes dancing. "I like a man to admit to some faults."

"Oh, I've plenty of them . . . and I could always discover a few more if it would please you," he said easily — and there was a degree of warmth in his tone that caused her to glance at him quickly. But she found nothing more than laughter in his eyes.

"I think you are trying to flirt with me, my lord," she said lightly. "I don't believe you have the least desire to please me . . . and I'm thankful for it."

"I'm a *very* eligible bachelor," he reminded her, smiling.

"I know . . . and I might be flattered if I didn't know that your bachelor days are almost at an end," she retorted.

He frowned slightly and glanced towards his lively sister. "Now I wonder what Victoria has been saying," he murmured.

"She happened to mention that you

are expecting to be married soon . . . it seems that congratulations are a little premature as nothing has been announced but I do wish you happy, Spenser," she told him carelessly and hoped he would not notice the slight tremor in her voice.

"Thank you . . . you are very kind," he said dryly.

She smiled at him sweetly and turned away to try once more to hold an intelligent conversation with the colonel. Spenser had no choice but to devote himself to Lady Nesbit and that terrifying old lady punished him for previous neglect by monopolising his attention for what remained of the meal.

Later on that evening the older members of the party retired to another room to play bridge and the rugs were thrown back in the drawing-room so that those who wished could dance to the music of a radiogram. More of Sophy's friends had arrived after dinner and Spenser had very little opportunity to talk to her. They were a very young crowd, he thought ruefully . . . noisy, demanding and a little overwhelming. He sought refuge for a few minutes on the small balcony that overlooked the pleasantly rural acres of Hampstead Heath.

Missing him immediately, Sophy eluded her friends and stepped out to the balcony, grateful for the cool and the quiet after the warmth and noise of the room.

"You aren't dancing," she said lightly as Spenser turned swiftly.

He smiled. "Neither are you."

She moved to his side and looked out over the Heath. "We are very lucky in our view, don't you think?"

"Very lucky . . . but it cannot compare with Staples, you know."

She smiled at him, touched by a certain tenderness in his voice when he spoke of his home. "You are much too insular," she chided him gently.

"Perhaps — but with very good cause, I think. You have never seen

Staples, Sophy . . . you must come down for a weekend and let me bore you with the beauties of my home. All my friends have to stand that test, I'm afraid."

She looked up at him with laughing eyes. "But you forget that we aren't friends, Spenser," she said lightly.

He laughed. "I can't think of you as an enemy." He held out his hand to her. "Dance with me," he suggested.

"Here . . . ?" she asked in some surprise.

He nodded. "Why not? I've danced on smaller floors in London nightclubs." He drew her into his arms and they began to move together to the music which flowed through the open window . . . slowly, their steps in perfect unison, their bodies melting into each other.

Sophy's heart was pounding so fiercely that she felt he must be aware of its tumult. This was a mistake, she thought ruefully . . . but she was too weak to rectify it. She might never again know the magic of dancing in his arms in the moonlight, the quiet of the still summer night lending a further enchantment to the moment.

They danced in silence. Sophy ceased to think and gave herself up to the delight of his nearness, the strength of his arms about her and the compelling magnetism of his personality. Spenser held her very close, surprised by her slender fragility and aware of a physical longing that startled him with its intensity. The soft perfume of her hair teased his senses and the yielding surrender of her body to his lead as they danced excited him unexpectedly.

Neither knew how it happened that their lips met and clung . . . briefly, fleetingly and yet so disturbingly. Sophy was the first to draw away, catching her breath on the realisation that a mere kiss could change her whole life . . . for in that moment she had known that she loved and would always love the man who had kissed her.

He raised his head and looked at her, smiling. She met his gaze with admirable steadiness . . . and he had no way of knowing how much it cost her to suppress the overwhelming tumult of heart and mind and appear both cool and collected.

He had been astonished by the sweetness of the lips beneath his own. Yet that kiss had been so fleeting that he could not be sure if she had responded at all — and her calmness implied that she had offered mere acceptance.

"Happy birthday, Sophy," he said slowly, thankful that he had an excuse on hand for that impulsive action.

She was grateful for the words even while her heart cried a protest that his kiss had been so meaningless, a token gesture. "Thank you . . . but you were almost too late," she returned with a composure that baffled the man who was unused to such casual acceptance of his kisses. "It's just ten minutes to midnight," she told him, pointing out the illuminated clock face of a distant church tower. She turned towards the open window. "I expect I am missed . . . and you, too. Are you coming in?"

"In a few moments . . ." He brought out his cigarette case and extracted a cigarette.

Sophy hesitated briefly. Then she nodded and slipped into the drawing-room where she was immediately claimed by Henry Mortimer. When Spenser had finished his cigarette, he followed her and saw that she was dancing with that young man, laughing up at him in response to some quip, and looking as though she had not a care in the world. It was impossible to suppose that she had given another thought to him or attached the least importance to the kiss they had exchanged. It did not matter, of course . . . indeed, he preferred that it should be so. But it was strange that he should feel both annoyed and resentful — just as though he had received a gentle but decisive rebuff at her hands . . .

Spenser decided to put off his return to Staples. His presence in town had brought a shower of invitations and he had other reasons for extending his visit. He wished to reach a definite conclusion about Georgina and he also wanted to keep an eye on Victoria's affairs. It did not matter that his sudden squiring of Georgina Winslow had aroused speculation among their friends. It did matter that he should have an opportunity to discover for himself how involved his sister was in an affair that she asserted to be non-existent. He had swiftly realised that Victoria was seeing more rather than less of Julius Marlowe for all her assurances to the contrary. If it was merely friendship then it was an odd kind of friendship for both Victoria and Marlowe seemed to ignore the existence of her husband.

It was puzzling that Luke did nothing to dissuade Victoria from spending so much of her time with another man . . . he could not really be deceived by the explanation that Marlowe was fascinated by his wife's beauty and was using her as a model for a planned exhibition of his work. It was even more puzzling and disturbing that Luke was seen less and less with Victoria as the days passed and seemed content to lead a life of his own that did not include his wife.

But the one item of gossip which might have disturbed Spenser very much more had not yet reached him . . . rumour that Victoria's husband had an interest of his own that explained his complacency — an interest in a woman he had known long before he met and married the lovely Victoria Chadwick.

Georgina might have enlightened him but she did not choose to distract him from the subject of his own marriage with concern for his sister's matrimonial problems . . . and it never crossed her mind that he would be interested in anything that also concerned Sophy Ransome.

She was feeling very confident about the outcome of Spenser's prolonged stay in town. She knew him too well to expect an eager and ardent courtship and she quite understood that love was not expected to enter into a marriage which would be more of a business contract than most women would care to accept. But Georgina meant to accept it. She prided herself on her commonsense and it had always been her ambition to marry Spenser . . . even in the days when she had believed herself to be in love with another man. Having been disillusioned by that unsatisfactory love affair, she was very willing to believe that marriage between close friends of long standing did not need the doubtful blessing of mutual loving for its success.

So the faint reserve and coolness in Spenser's attitude did not trouble her at all. She understood that he was not yet ready to commit himself and she was much too sensible to resent the knowledge that he was vetting her thoroughly before making up his mind. She approved his caution. Marriage for any Chadwick was considered to be a lifelong commitment and he must be very sure of his ground before asking any woman to marry him. It would be difficult for anyone to fault her eligibility, thought Georgina with serene confidence and, knowing that he had a certain amount of affection for her and enjoyed her company, she was content to wait for the proposal that she knew he would eventually utter . . .

It was very natural and only to be expected that Spenser and Sophy should encounter each other from time to time while he remained in London. Their meetings were brief and too casual to be memorable — unless one chose to remember.

Nightclubs, restaurants and lively parties were not conducive to any more than casual conversation — he was always with Georgina or other friends and Sophy was usually involved with a party of her own whenever they met.

Those encounters left little impression on Spenser's mind. Only the occasional fleeting thought of her troubled him and perhaps he unconsciously sought to suppress those for the rebuff he had received still rankled slightly. It had been the second rebuff, he reminded himself in some irritation . . . for all her lightness of manner and laughing eyes she had decidedly refused his friendship. She was holding him at arms' length . . . not through a feminine caution but because she continued to view him with dislike and contempt for all the easy and careless friendliness of her manner when they met.

He accepted those occasional meetings as inevitable and refused to attach any importance to them. He did not manoeuvre them or seek her out in any way for he was much too proud to risk a further rebuff at the hands of a woman who disliked him . . . it was obvious that she meant to keep him at a distance and he told himself that he was content to remain there . . .

Sophy did not welcome those brief encounters for she was trying hard to put him out of her mind and heart . . . and it was alarming to discover that a mere glimpse of him across a room had the power to send her heart somersaulting, leaving her sick and shaken. She took refuge quite instinctively in a pretence of indifference . . . and gained no satisfaction whatsoever from the realisation that he neither noticed nor felt her lack of warmth or interest.

She had not forgotten Victoria's comments on his marriage plans and it seemed that they were more or less definite. He always seemed to be with Georgina Winslow whenever she saw him and there was no mistaking the air of confident satisfaction that emanated from the beautiful and very sophisticated woman. His courtship was apparently well under way and running smoothly and Sophy woke every morning with the ridiculous dread of reading the announcement of his engagement in *The Times*.

There was nothing she could do

to prevent it, of course. Obviously he would marry one day if he did not marry Georgina Winslow. As she would never be his bride she must face the unpalatable fact that some other woman would take the place that she could not help foolishly feeling was really her own.

For Sophy, loving was synonymous with the longing to spend the rest of her life with the man she loved. But she knew only too well that it was an impossible dream. She was not so ineligible . . . marriage between them would be wholly acceptable in the eyes of their world . . . but Spenser so obviously did not even see her as a woman to interest him let alone as a possible wife that it was the height of folly to allow herself to dream and only led to heartache.

She despised the weakness which had led her into loving a man who did not appear to give her a second thought. But she could not stop loving him. Without the least encouragement to do so she continued to ache for his notice without cessation . . . and to pretend a serene indifference to the very existence of Spenser, Earl of Cleveland.

As it happened, if she had attempted to cast out lures in his direction her efforts would only have served to add fuel to the gossip that linked her name with that of Luke Cardigan. It would generally have been believed that she sought to throw dust in everyone's eyes and particularly the eyes of Victoria.

Fortunately for her peace of mind, she was completely unaware of the gossip. It had never occurred to her that the warmth of understanding she enjoyed with Luke could be open to misconstruction. They had been friends since she was little more than a child . . . she had always regarded him much in the light of a brother and she had been delighted with the result of her first and only attempt at matchmaking. Luke had fallen in love with Victoria at first sight and within weeks it had appeared that Victoria's emotions were just as deeply involved. She had welcomed the announcement of their engagement and looked forward to their wedding with almost as much eager and delighted anticipation as if it had been her own.

It seemed both right and natural that Luke should seek her out on social occasions if Victoria should temporarily desert him . . . equally natural that a chance meeting should lead to a drink or a meal together . . . and just as natural that she should feel free to call on her friends at any time and never be disconcerted if Luke happened to be alone when she called. Perhaps it was foolishly naive but she did not realise that the most innocent encounter could be used against her by any unscrupulous person who wished to create scandal . . . and Luke, usually the most thoughtful and farseeing of men, was so confident that all the world must know how deeply he loved his wife that he was blind and deaf to the speculation that circulated about his relationship with Sophy. Both would have been appalled by the rumour that Luke was as anxious for his freedom as his wife seemed to be since she had become involved with Julius Marlowe.

It was true that Sophy was spending more time in Luke's company of late . . . she was his only confidante, the only one to whom he could unburden his growing anxiety about the state of his marriage and the only person who could convince him that he was making a mountain out of a molehill — except for Victoria who was becoming more and more remote and increasingly difficult to talk to. Sophy was an intimate friend of Victoria's and she could be trusted not to offer empty platitudes. If Sophy said firmly that Victoria was not likely to do anything foolish, that the affair would fizzle out if he avoided making an issue of it and thus forced his proud wife into impulsive and reckless action, then Sophy was to be believed. When Sophy assured him that he was the only man who mattered to Victoria and that her flirtatiousness was merely the thoughtless behaviour of a spoiled and very young girl who had never been taught to consider the feelings of anyone but herself, then Luke could allow himself to be reassured and was able to view Victoria's hurtful attitude with the tender indulgence of a man too much in love and too wary of losing the most precious thing in his life to exert his authority as a husband.

It was Sophy's sincerity that carried so much weight . . . and she was wholly sincere in believing that Victoria loved Luke. She was baffled and bewildered by her friend's foolish affair with Marlowe but she did not believe it was anything more than flirtation, due to thoughtlessness and a careless disregard for convention. She had no way of knowing that Victoria was deeply unhappy and convinced that Luke had never loved her. Her friend concealed her feelings too well and was much too proud to admit openly to any lack in her marriage. In any case, Sophy would have found it difficult to accept that Victoria doubted the depth and strength of Luke's feelings . . . it was so obvious that his wife was the be-all and end-all of Luke's existence.

If she had known and appreciated Victoria's growing resentment of her husband's undemanding indulgence she might not have cautioned him so consistently against tackling Victoria on the subject of her friendship with Marlowe. All unconsciously, she was doing them both a disservice — the last thing she could have wanted for either of her friends . . .

Victoria had always been inclined to regard Luke's affection for Sophy with an indulgent eye. She knew how long they had known each other and had never been given any cause to doubt the innocence of their relationship. It was Julius who first planted the seed of suspicion, so skilfully that she did not realise that it was deliberately done. He was growing impatient with the girl who hesitated on the brink of surrender for so long. He wanted her more than he had ever wanted any woman . . . it was not a question of loving but of refusing to believe that the woman existed who could resist his clever, subtle persuasions. So far Victoria had resisted . . . it was frustrating and infuriating and the first ripples of gossip concerning her husband and Sophy Ransome presented him with a weapon he did not hesitate to use. He had a very poor opinion of Luke Cardigan . . . as he had of any man with a beautiful wife who did not guard her carefully from the attentions of other men. He did not care if there was truth or not in the gossip . . . he was merely concerned with assuaging his desire for Victoria by fair or foul means. Marriage was never in his mind . . . he had no wish to appear in a divorce court and had always extricated himself from an affair in time to avoid that unpleasantness. Nor did he have any wish to exchange the wife he had for another . . . Melanie suited him very well and had long since ceased to care whether or not he was faithful to her provided he kept her in the comfort she enjoyed and did not interfere with her upbringing of their three young children.

At first, Victoria was amused that Julius or anyone else could suppose it possible that Luke and Sophy were involved in anything more than friendship. She prided herself on her perception and she had never sensed the existence of any feeling but affection and friendship between them. Luke was always open about his meetings with Sophy . . . and she never looked conscious if Luke's name was mentioned or went out of her way to monopolise his attention at any time. But those seemingly casual remarks made by Julius were not easily forgotten . . . for some reason they recurred to her mind again and again. Linked with her conviction that Luke had never really loved her but married her on the tide

of infatuation which had soon ebbed
and with the awareness that Sophy
possessed an appeal that captivated
most men, it was not very long before
she began to wonder if Luke had
discovered too late that he should have
married Sophy. It was an explanation
for the rapid cooling of his ardency,
the careless indifference to her feelings,
the indulgent tolerance with which he
viewed her dealings with Julius. In the
early days of their marriage she had
resented his efforts to impose certain
restrictions on her way of life and she
had made it clear to him that she would
not tolerate any man's hand on her rein
. . . could she blame Luke if he had
come to share her attitude to marriage?
Perhaps he was now content to allow
them to drift, to go their own ways
. . . even to allow her to take a lover
as long as she turned a blind eye to
any similar indiscretion on his part? It
was the kind of marriage that existed all
too often in their world . . . the kind of
marriage she had once supposed to be

the ideal. But she had learned that it was not the kind of marriage that she wanted . . . and she was terrified that it was too late to build successfully on the crumbling foundation of the last few months of her life with Luke.

She refused to accept that he was lost to her . . . but she was very much on the alert for any evidence that he was consoling himself with Sophy while she foolishly encouraged Julius to dance attendance on her. She would not be sorry to break with Julius . . . it had been amusing, even exciting, to lead him on but she was finding it more and more difficult to handle him and she was becoming a little afraid that he would take by force what she would not surrender willingly. She had originally started the affair in an attempt to make Luke jealous — her failure to do so seemed an indication that he had never cared enough to be jealous and so there was no point in going on with a game that was threatening to become a battle for supremacy.

Of course, there was no truth in the silly piece of gossip that Julius had passed on . . . but it was always possible that Luke was jealous and had sought to punish her by seeing so much of Sophy that gossip was inevitable and must eventually reach her ears, she told herself hopefully — and marvelled that her pride had crumbled so completely that she could snatch at even that small grain of comfort . . .

Pride was all very well but it was no solace for an aching heart.

7

SPENSER regarded his companion somewhat dispassionately, deciding that he had seldom known her look more lovely. She wore a flame-coloured sheath that revealed the gentle swell of her breasts and bared her slender shoulders, emphasizing the narrow waist and sleek hips. Her only ornament was the diamond sunburst pendant that nestled at her throat and sparkled as vividly as her eyes.

He wished that he truly appreciated her beauty, her sophisticated elegance and the smiling invitation in her eyes ... but she did not inspire him with anything more than the ordinary affection of long and familiar friendship. He supposed the fault must lie with him and wondered what quirk it was in his nature that made him so very difficult to please.

The evening was pleasant without being at all memorable — although he did not doubt that Georgina hoped it would be an evening to remember. He played his part well enough and knew it was no more than pretence. They danced and he held her close and murmured the foolish nonsense that she expected even if she did not believe . . . and despised himself for conforming to her code. They ate and drank and talked lightly and emptily . . . and danced again.

He was not a cold man and the slender body in his arms could quicken his blood but it was no more than fleeting desire. With each succeeding day he had found himself more reluctant to propose marriage to this beautiful and very confident woman . . . and this was his last evening in town. He must return to Staples and the work he had neglected even if he came back to London again very soon.

Perhaps it was her confidence that chilled and repelled him for she did not even pretend to be ignorant of his purpose in paying her such marked attentions. Her expectation of his proposal was in her eyes, her smile, her voice, her easy acceptance of him and her gracious willingness to be available whenever he chose to call, to telephone or to escort her to various functions. It seemed that she would marry him without hesitation and he supposed he should be gratified by her willingness. He did not suppose that she loved him but she would certainly be exactly the kind of wife he sought . . . if he ignored the absence of a certain quality of warmth, generosity and a readiness to give herself completely to the ensuring of his happiness.

Quite unbidden, the image of a fair and slender girl leaped to his mind . . . a girl that he seemed to see at every turn, wherever he went, of late. It was an exaggeration, of course — many, many times the cool, slim blonde across a room, the other side of a street, in the corner of a restaurant, on a passing bus or reflected in the mirror of a hotel bar proved to be anyone but Sophy Ransome. It was merely the memory of her that haunted him . . . and he was not at all pleased about it.

He had not seen her for several days . . . through one cause or another their paths simply had not crossed. And he had missed her . . . It was very strange but quite true. He had missed the odd little stab of pleasure that the sight of her had brought him and he had missed the sound of her cool, provocative voice with its ready challenge and he had missed the swift, sudden laughter in her green eyes that he had seldom failed to ignite no matter how hard she tried to keep him at distance.

There was a risk to staying in town any longer that he could not afford . . . he did not wish to discover that he was falling in love with a chit of a girl who would make him a most unsuitable wife even if he could persuade her into marriage — which he very much doubted.

But he scorned the thought even as it entered his head . . . falling in love, indeed! Love did not exist except in the minds of fools and romantics — and he was neither! He was past the age of such folly . . . a man of thirty-five did not fall in love for the first time with a woman he scarcely knew. A man of thirty-five did not fall in love, damn it! A fine fool he would look after all he had voiced so cynically on the subject of love. One woman was much like another . . . if he wanted to fancy himself in love so that marriage would be more palatable to him then he would be wise to choose Georgina as the recipient of such a foolish emotion. Georgina was the ideal choice and he ought to sweep her into marriage before he could make a fool of himself over an outspoken, intolerant and impertinent chit . . .

It was not the first time he had thought of Sophy Ransome only to see her in the flesh moments later.

He should have been inured to such coincidences but he found that he could still experience that tiny shock about his heart at the sight of her. She came towards their table in all innocence, quite unaware of him, scanning the room beyond — and Spenser half-rose in his seat to claim her notice, delighted anticipation in his smile and eyes, realizing in that moment that she was already dearer to him than he had suspected.

Sophy saw him . . . and hesitated. Supposing him to have left town, the shock of seeing him so unexpectedly when for once he had not been in the forefront of her mind, sent her heart leaping into her throat and her mind scurrying in panic-stricken circles. She knew a painful awareness of his beautiful companion and wondered drearily when that engagement would be announced and so end her torment of apprehension and hope.

Terrified of betraying her swift, glad delight or that fierce, stabbing jealousy which consumed her, she could not trust herself to pause by his table, to speak to him. She granted him a cool little nod of acknowledgement and passed by, blind and deaf to everything but the pounding of her heart, desperately hoping that he could not sense the wild tumult of her blood or the sudden, alarming weakness of loving and wanting that melted her very bones. She saw Luke waiting for her at a secluded table and she hurried towards him thankfully, not suspecting for a moment that she had hurt and offended the one man whose friendship and affection she desired so much . . .

Spenser's lips were white and his eyes held a dangerous glitter as he sank back into his seat, looking after the girl who had brushed aside the compliment of his notice. In his fury he was guilty of all the arrogance that had been laid at his door so often. He was unreasonably angry that she had dismissed him so lightly and so offensively. He had never been snubbed in his life but she had snubbed him — deliberately, humiliatingly and without cause. His anger blared as she went on her way, the very coolness of her self-possession an added affront to his pride.

Georgina had watched the incident with interest and more than a little suspicion. She also watched the straight, uncompromising figure of Sophy Ransome as she made her way to that quiet corner where a man awaited her . . . a man who rose eagerly to his feet at her approach and held out his hand to her . . . a man that Georgina recognized with a sense of satisfaction.

She looked at Spenser and then checked the faintly malicious words that she had been about to utter. She had never seen that particular look in his eyes before but she immediately recognised the danger of drawing that unmistakable fury to herself.

Her eyes narrowed thoughtfully. She knew Sophy Ransome, of course, but they were little more than casual acquaintances and she had never interested herself in a young woman who was not one of her particular circle of friends. Suddenly she *was* interested . . .

Georgina was not at all pleased by the thought that she had a rival to Spenser's affections at this late date. It was really galling in view of the girl's youth and virtual insignificance. Yet she apparently had contrived to interest Spenser to some extent — and Georgina would give a great deal to know how extensive an interest it was!

She did not really believe that Sophy Ransome was much of a threat to her ambitions. Spenser would scarcely contemplate marriage with a girl so unsuited to him but a temporary attraction might deflect him from what she felt sure had been his original purpose in coming up to town and staying so much longer than anyone had expected. She had waited a long time for her moment of triumph . . . she had felt that it was drawing near and she had been sufficiently confident to hint to her delighted parents and a few intimate friends that she would soon become the Countess of Cleveland. She had no desire to suffer humiliation because of a fleeting and rather foolish attraction that Sophy Ransome might possess for him . . .

She said softly: "Poor child . . . I'm afraid you embarrassed her, Spenser."

He glanced at her swiftly, coldly. "What do you mean?"

"I expect you are almost the last person she would choose to run into . . . in the circumstances," she told him lightly.

He frowned. "I can't think of any circumstances which would make it embarrassing for Sophy Ransome and myself to meet by chance in a public restaurant."

"You are Victoria's brother," she reminded him gently.

"And she is Victoria's friend," he returned coolly.

Georgina hesitated. It was the merest pause, cleverly conveying a reluctance to even hint at the gossip that was currently circulating. "I'm afraid she has not been a very good friend to Victoria," she said quietly, regretfully . . . and glanced deliberately in the direction of the table where Sophy sat with Luke Cardigan.

He followed her gaze, as she had intended, and for the first time he noticed Luke. His brother-in-law was absorbed in his companion, leaning forward and speaking with obvious urgency, his hand resting on the slim fingers of the girl who faced him . . . the girl whose expression seemed to convey the unmistakable warmth of understanding and affection.

Spenser was jolted . . . not so much by the evidence of an intimacy he had never suspected but by the glow in Sophy's eyes as she listened to Luke and the tremulous sweetness of her smile. Abruptly he realised that Sophy might have had very good reason for not wishing to meet him on this particular occasion — and he was filled with a blind, fierce tumult of emotion in which desire and contempt, disappointment and anger were inextricably mixed.

Certainly it was none of his business in the ordinary way if Sophy Ransome chose to conduct an affair with a married man — but it was very much his business when that man was married to his own sister!

He was angry with Luke who had so cleverly convinced him of a non-existent devotion to Victoria, conveyed a patient, trusting acceptance of his wife's youthful indiscretions, contrived to win everyone's sympathy while it was obviously to his advantage that Victoria should weary of their marriage and look elsewhere for the happiness that he had perhaps deliberately denied her. Spenser did not pause to wonder why Luke had married Victoria in the first place if he cared for Sophy Ransome . . . nor did he pause to remember his conviction that Victoria had married on the strength of an infatuation that had not survived more than a few weeks of close intimacy with her new husband. Nor did it strike him as ironic that he should be so concerned to protect his sister from the hurt and humiliation of speculation about her marriage when she seemed so indifferent to public opinion for her own part. It seemed to him very natural that Victoria should have chosen to flaunt a meaningless flirtation before the world rather than have it supposed that she was an unhappy, neglected and jealous wife.

He felt nothing but contempt for the girl who had furthered her interest in a man by pretending affection for his wife, he told himself harshly. He realised that he had been ready to endow Sophy Ransome with all kinds of excellent qualities, not least among them being an integrity which must set her above the tawdriness of an illicit affair. He reminded himself scornfully that he knew nothing of the girl. Perhaps other women's husbands were her speciality, he thought grimly, remembering how little encouragement she had offered him — a most eligible and not unattractive bachelor!

He wrenched his attention from the couple who were so engrossed in each other. With a natural desire to rid Georgina's mind of any suspicion that she might pass on to others, he said carelessly: "I believe you mistake the matter, my dear." His tone was decisive for all its casualness.

Georgina sent him a smile of understanding. "Oh, very likely," she agreed lightly. "Appearances can be so deceptive . . . and I believe they were friends before he met Victoria. In fact, I'm told that it was Sophy Ransome who first introduced them to each other."

"Indeed?" he countered indifferently. "Then there is nothing remarkable in their intimacy."

"Except that it is more marked of late, perhaps," she murmured. "No, don't scowl at me, Spenser," she added swiftly, placatingly. "I am no gossip — but I have noticed one or two things for myself. I've known Victoria since she was a child, after all . . . naturally I've been a little concerned about the whole thing from the beginning." She smiled at him suddenly, warmly. "When you came up to town I fancied it was your intention to put things right — but I suppose it isn't as simple as that."

"I've yet to be convinced that there is anything to put right," he said smoothly. "Luke is on good terms with a young woman who happens to be Victoria's friend as well as his own . . . and Victoria is indulging in a mild and harmless flirtation as she has done all her adult life."

"Every marriage has its teething troubles," she agreed lightly. "But I can't really believe that Victoria enjoys the attentions of a man like Marlowe. I *can* understand the attitude that what appeals to the gander might be equally palatable for the goose!" She paused, glancing briefly at his expressionless face, and then she added quietly: "It seems that Luke and Sophy have always been very close — and a young bride can be very sensitive about these things."

"Oh, I don't doubt that they are both being a little foolish," he said carelessly. "But these misunderstandings have a habit of settling themselves — all the more quickly without interference from well-meaning friends or relatives," he added, a little grimly.

"My dear! I wouldn't dream of interfering," she protested indignantly. "After all, they are not children."

He was silent, his glance straying again across the room. It was Sophy's turn to talk and Luke's to listen, an intent expression in his eyes.

A period of deafness in his childhood, caused by an accidental kick from his opponent in a rugby game, had taught Spenser the art of lip-reading and it was a skill he had not forgotten. Despising himself for doing so, he watched the movement of Sophy's lips . . .

She was saying: " . . . divorce her, Luke. You could never be happy . . . "

He removed his gaze abruptly, discovering he did not really wish to have complete evidence of her despicable behaviour. But he had seen enough to know that she was urging Luke to obtain his freedom . . . and it did not need undue intelligence to realize that she was anxious to marry the man herself. He had no sympathy for a girl who had innocently introduced the man she loved to a friend only to find herself temporarily cast aside while he rushed into marriage with the other woman. He did not care that she might have suffered heartache and humiliation . . . nor did he blame his sister for taking her happiness at the expense of her friend's feelings. All was fair in love . . . and Victoria loved her husband however foolishly she might flirt with other men. Luke had always seemed to him to be a weak man . . . he had been putty in Victoria's hands. He was obviously just as weak where Sophy was concerned . . . probably incapable of loving her or anyone else, he was equally incapable of telling her so and drifted with the tide while he waited for circumstances to settle matters one way or the other. He would not take steps to divorce Victoria, of course — that would be too decisive an action for such a man, Spenser thought contemptuously. He had allowed her to do as she pleased because he had no idea how to handle her . . . and now he was allowing Sophy to run away with the idea that he would secure his freedom and marry her because he had no idea how to extricate himself from an awkward situation.

Spenser's anger and contempt were all the greater because he had always liked Luke . . . and he could not even think about Sophy Ransome without wishing to lay violent hands on her because he had experienced a sudden revelation where she was concerned. He thrust away the thought that she was the one woman he could have loved. She had deceived him with her warmth and candour and light-hearted appeal . . . as she had no doubt deceived many others. He realized now that she had always been on the defensive where he was concerned . . . and that was natural enough in view of the fact that he was Victoria's brother. She had been afraid of becoming involved with him for she might have inadvertently betrayed her feeling for Luke and then all her plans would have been doomed to failure.

They still were, he thought grimly. For he would not allow anyone to destroy Victoria's happiness and Luke would settle down and accept the inevitable once Sophy had been removed from his sphere. He might be incapable of ending that association but Spenser Chadwick was not!

"Shall we dance . . . ?" Georgina suggested tentatively, hoping to deflect his attention from the couple who absorbed it.

He had been so preoccupied that he had almost forgotten the woman by his side. He did not want Georgina to suppose that he attached so much importance to the matter. He rose immediately. "Certainly . . . " He smiled down at her as he led her out to the dance floor. "Forgive me . . . I didn't meant to be discourteous."

"But you never are, Spenser," she assured him as they began to dance. "I've often wondered what you are really thinking and feeling behind that unfailing shield of good manners. I really believe that a few moments ago you were wishing me a hundred miles away," she added teasingly.

Because he was tormented by the memory of another woman in his arms — slender, fragile and so very desirable — he said abruptly, fiercely attempting to erase the image: "Indeed I was . . . I wished you at Staples, Georgina."

She raised an enquiring eyebrow. "At Staples! But why?"

Deliberately he tightened his hold on

her slim waist. "Because I am more at ease in my own surroundings, I suppose . . . and might not find it so difficult to ask you to marry me."

She looked up at him swiftly, careful to conceal that leaping triumph. "Is this a proposal, Spenser?" she asked lightly.

"I must be very ham-handed if you are in doubt," he said ruefully, plunging even deeper. "But I've had no practice at the business, you see."

Georgina laughed softly. "Well, I'm glad of that, anyway."

They were passing the quiet corner where Luke and Sophy sat . . . Spenser looked over his partner's head at the table and met Sophy's eyes. She looked away quickly in confusion . . . and he hardened his heart which had threatened to weaken at the sight of her small and inexpressibly dear face.

"*Will* you marry me?" he asked and brushed Georgina's smooth cheek with his lips.

Her hand stole from his broad

shoulder to the thick tendrils of hair at the nape of his neck. "Of course I will," she murmured softly. "No one if not you, I promise."

He was suddenly alarmed. Surely she was not in love with him . . . that was the last thing he wanted. It was bad enough to be denying all his instincts in this way without taking on the extra burden of knowing that he was betraying a woman who loved him.

He held her away from him and looked down at her steadily. "You do realise that I'm not in love with you, Georgina," he said quietly. "I can't deceive you on that point . . . it would be impossible for me to pretend."

She smiled and gave a little shrug. She was feminine enough to be piqued by the blunt words . . . after all, no woman liked to be told that she had failed to inspire the least degree of love in a man. But she was grateful for his honesty . . . it would make things so much easier in the future.

"And equally impossible for me, my

dear," she assured him firmly. "We are very fortunate, you know . . . we should be able to build a very successful life together knowing there are no foolish emotional complications to make things difficult. It's very rare for any marriage to start off on such an excellent and sensible basis."

Cold-blooded to the extreme, Spenser thought with a shock of dismay as he heard the words. He had always supposed that he preferred a woman to be practical and level-headed but he was appalled to discover that Georgina was viewing their marriage much as she would a proposed business venture. What on earth had possessed him to propose to her . . . he must have been temporarily out of his senses!

It was much too late to retract. With a sinking heart, he realised that he had invited a lifetime of empty, bleak loneliness and perpetual despair . . . but he was committed. Georgina would never release him, he knew — and it was quite impossible for him to escape now that the fatal words had been uttered . . .

"You expected this, I think," he said slowly, deciding to meet frankness with frankness.

She laughed — and now the triumph was obvious for she had gained what she had wanted and she knew he was not a man to withdraw even if he had only asked her because the discovery of Sophy Ransome's preference for another man had caught him on the raw. "In common with everyone else, Spenser," she said lightly.

"Yes . . . yes, I suppose so," he agreed, a little harshly . . . and remembered that Sophy had also expected him to marry Georgina. In different circumstances he might have assumed it to be the reason why she had refused to regard him as anything more than a casual acquaintance for on several occasions he had suspected that she liked him more than she would admit.

He could not help hoping that she

would be a little dismayed when the engagement was announced . . . even though he knew it to be a forlorn hope . . .

Sophy did not need to read the announcement in *The Times*. She had only to see the glowing triumph in Georgina Winslow's eyes to know that Spenser had finally asked her to marry him and had been accepted. Involuntarily her hands clenched — so tightly that the knuckles gleamed and her nails were forced fiercely into her palms. She did not even notice. She stared blankly at the tall figure of Spenser Chadwick as he threaded his way back through the tables with Georgina's hand lying lightly but possessively on his arm.

An icy hand gripped her heart as she thought of the man she loved taking that cold and ruthless and unmistakably ambitious woman to wife. She had accepted the impossibility of marrying him herself but she desperately wanted his happiness . . . and that he would

185

never find in such a marriage, she thought bleakly. Georgina cared nothing for the man. She only wanted the prestige and the standing and the financial security that he could offer. Sophy scarcely knew the woman but she knew these things by instinct.

There must be a way to prevent that marriage — she could not let him marry such a woman. She did not believe he loved Georgina Winslow . . . he had spoken of his need to marry coldly and he had admitted frankly that there was no question of loving. Perhaps he was incapable of loving any woman but he still had the right of every human being to be loved! And Sophy loved him and she was prepared to go to any lengths to secure some measure of happiness and comfort for him . . .

8

"WHAT is it, Sophy?" Luke asked in concern, seeing the desperation in her eyes and the lack of colour in her small face.

She came back to him slowly, finding it difficult to associate him with her wild, impossible thoughts. "I'm sorry . . . what were you saying?" she said vaguely.

"Are you all right?" he demanded, pouring fresh wine into her glass and handing it to her. "You look . . . I don't know — not ill, exactly. A bit shattered."

"Do I?" She managed a shaky laugh. "It's nothing . . . a touch of faintness, perhaps. It's so hot — stuffy — I'm developing a wicked headache."

"I'll take you home," he said decisively and gestured to the waiter who had attended their table.

"I'm sorry, Luke . . . I've ruined the evening," she said regretfully.

"Nonsense!" he declared. He took her hands and held them very tightly. "You're a great comfort to me, Sophy . . . I think I'd be in utter despair if I didn't have you to reduce my mountains to molehills."

She looked at him, wondering how she had the temerity to advise him or anyone else on how to run their affairs when she was so hopeless at managing her own. A clever woman would have known just how to attract Spenser Chadwick . . . and might by now have been celebrating an engagement in Georgina Winslow's place. But she was not clever. She had allowed herself to be frightened by her first awareness of his physical magnetism . . . and she had been running away from him ever since, knowing herself to be too vulnerable and terrified of being hurt and disappointed.

"Supposing I'm wrong . . . quite wrong," she said slowly. "Supposing

I've given you all the wrong advice?"

He shook his head. "I don't think so," he said confidently. "If I'd followed my instincts I'd have beaten poor Victoria and confined her to her room until Julius Marlowe was forgotten . . . cave-man tactics. They would never have worked with Victoria, of course."

"They might have been very effective. A truly feminine woman likes a man to be masterful," she said thoughtfully.

"Not Victoria! She has never been told yea or nay by anyone in all her life," he said ruefully.

"Then that is just what she needs!" Sophy told him decisively, reaching for her bag and rising to her feet.

Luke stared at her in surprise. "Are you serious?"

"Of course I am! It would do her a great deal of good to learn that she can't ride roughshod over you or anyone else . . . show her that you mean to be master and your problems will be over. Try it," she advised him.

"I'm going to powder my nose . . . wait for me in the foyer, will you?"

He looked after her in bewilderment. For weeks she had been advising him to give Victoria her head without restraint, to swallow everything without complaint or criticism. Even this very evening when, feeling that he had almost reached the end of his tether, he had wearily concluded that it was hopeless to go on, she had urged him to dismiss the idea of divorce and assured him that he could never be happy without Victoria. It was perfectly true — but how long could a man live with the bleakness of knowing that he had completely failed to make a woman happy and contented.

He wondered if Sophy could be right. He seemed to be getting nowhere by assuming a passive rôle . . . it could scarcely do much harm if he finally made a stand. He did not contemplate beating his wife, of course. It was impossible for him to harm a hair of her lovely head, he thought wryly.

Nor could he lock her in her room . . . she would simply throw a tantrum and disturb the entire household. But he could and would tell her bluntly that she must end her association with Marlowe, resign herself to the humdrum domesticity of being his wife and the mother of his children — or agree to a divorce so that they could both look for happiness with someone else. He hoped to shock her into the realisation that he was very necessary to her . . . but he thought it much more likely that she would leap at the suggestion of a divorce . . .

She was in bed and asleep when he arrived home and he did not have the heart to disturb her. She looked so very young and innocent, her beautiful hair streaming across the pillows, long lashes forming a crescent on her smooth cheeks and her mouth curving softly in a half-smile as she enjoyed her dreams. He bent over the bed and touched his lips very gently to her brow. She stirred and murmured something but she did not waken. With a sigh, he turned away . . . and knew he would need to harden his heart if he meant to carry out his new resolution . . .

She slept late and did not join him for breakfast. He debated the wisdom of cancelling his appointments for the morning . . . and was not sorry to have a ready excuse for postponing his showdown with Victoria. He wrote a brief note and left the house to keep his first appointment.

Victoria came down some ten minutes later. She was disappointed to find that Luke had already eaten and left for the office. It was not an unusual circumstance but this morning her heart sank a little for she could not help wondering if he was deliberately avoiding her. They had scarcely seen each other for days. She was mostly to blame, of course . . . but it did seem that Luke no longer cared to spend any of his time in her company. His note did nothing to lift her sudden depression . . . it was brief and decidedly curt, she thought in dismay. He wished to talk to her and would be obliged if she would cancel any arrangements she might have that afternoon . . . he expected to be home for lunch. He had merely signed his name as though they were strangers.

She had no appetite for her breakfast and merely pushed the food about her plate. She was vaguely alarmed. What was it that Luke had to say to her . . . that was so important it could not wait beyond the morning? Only a fool could have missed the significance of the curt note which contained none of the affection and tenderness that a wife might be expected to look for in a note from her husband.

Was this the end, she wondered bleakly. Did he mean to tell her that their marriage was finished — that he loved Sophy and wanted his freedom for her sake? Her mind seethed with all the suspicion and jealousy that Julius had aroused with his seemingly casual words and which had been fostered by her own sudden awareness of the understanding which existed between Luke and Sophy. She knew that they had been seeing each other frequently in recent days. She knew, too, that Luke had been troubled about something . . . he had looked at her occasionally as though he was about to confide in her and always he had turned away without speaking.

She could not even comfort herself with the thought that Luke might have been hurt by her association with Julius and had turned to Sophy for consolation. He had never really loved her, she thought unhappily . . . he had always been too tolerant, too indulgent, too patient with her whims and caprices. A man in love did not allow his wife to play fast and loose with his happiness and peace of mind.

Had he always loved Sophy? If so, why hadn't he married her? Because she did not care for him — or because his feelings had not crystallised until he found himself married to a woman who was so very different to Sophy? Or had he fallen in love with Sophy only after their marriage, Victoria wondered drearily . . . because she had failed him in so many ways. Might he have come to love her in truth if she had behaved differently, allowed him to know how dear he was to her, adapted herself to his ideal of all that a wife should be?

Her mind was running around in circles . . . and she turned thankfully to her brother when he walked into the room, unannounced.

"Spenser! I didn't expect to see you this morning! I thought you were going home."

"I am . . . but I wanted to see you first." He looked down at her, noting her pallor. "I want to talk to you."

Her eyes widened. "Everyone wants to talk to me today!" she exclaimed, concealing apprehension with pretended lightness. "I hope you haven't come to plead Luke's case for him . . . I know you like him but that is carrying friendship too far!"

He pulled out a chair and sat down. "So you do know," he said slowly, heavily.

Her heart plummeted. With an effort, she managed to laugh. "Do you think I am blind . . . or a fool — or both? Have you eaten, by the way?"

"Yes . . . yes, of course — hours ago!" he said impatiently. He picked up a knife and studied it thoughtfully. "Is it pride . . . or simply indifference, Victoria?"

"My God . . . if you think I *care* . . . !" She rose abruptly, struggling to control her emotions. "Let him make a fool of himself," she said in a strangled voice.

He was silent for a moment. Then he said quietly: "I'm sorry, my dear . . . this isn't pleasant for you."

"Even if I've asked for it?" she retorted harshly. "Like everyone else you think I've driven him into her arms by my friendship with Julius. Well, you're wrong! This . . . this thing with Sophy started long before I met

Julius Marlowe."

"I suspected that," he told her grimly.

She stared at him. "It must be more obvious than I thought — unless . . . oh, of course! You want Sophy, too, don't you? Did she tell you that she has other plans . . . plans that include my husband?" she demanded bitterly.

"What makes you think I'm interested in Sophy Ransome?" he returned sharply.

She shrugged. "Intuition."

"You are mistaken," he told her harshly. "I am going to marry Georgina."

She looked up quickly. "It's settled?"

"Yes . . . it's settled."

There was something in his tone that brought dismay to her heart. "Oh, Spenser," she said wearily. "You are as much of an idiot as I am."

Irritated, he retorted sharply: "You are married to Luke and should have made sure that you didn't lose him . . . I knew you were reckless but I didn't believe you could be stupid as well."

"You don't understand . . . " She broke off, shrugging. It would be impossible to explain how things had stood between her and Luke since the earliest days of their marriage. "I suppose I should offer my congratulations . . . but I *can't*, Spenser! I think you are making a terrible mistake!"

"We must all make our own mistakes . . . and pay for them," he said indifferently. "Do you care to come back to Staples with me, Victoria? It is still your home and you will be spared much of the inevitable unpleasantness."

"But . . . Luke . . . "

"Won't it simplify things all round?"

She hesitated. It seemed such a final step to take . . . but what else could she do? She could not face Luke . . . she knew she would humble herself, grovel if necessary, beg him to stay with her and promise all manner of things — and she still had her pride. If Luke wanted Sophy — and it seemed that he did if Spenser was so sure that divorce was in her husband's mind — then she would not stand in his way. Her heart was breaking but Luke must not know it . . . kind, gentle, considerate Luke who could not help loving another woman any more than she could help loving him and who would certainly sacrifice his happiness if she allowed him to know how much he meant to her. How could he know, she thought despondently . . . she had been so selfish, so wilful, so petulant and childish in her dealings with him. She had given so little and taken so much in return. She had put her own wishes, her own pleasures, her own interest before Luke from the very beginning. How could she blame him for wanting his freedom?

Spenser studied her thoughtfully and then said with a challenge in his voice: "What is it? Don't you wish to be so far from Marlowe?"

She detected a faint sneer and her

eyes flashed. "Julius? Julius has nothing to do with it! I told him last night that I would not see him again . . . I should have done it weeks ago."

He did not doubt the ring of sincerity in the words. "It might have averted this business," he agreed quietly.

She shook her head. "I don't think so . . . delayed it, perhaps. I can't compete with Sophy — she is everything I could never be," she said wistfully.

"You can still admire her!" he exclaimed in surprise.

"Do you blame Sophy? I don't. I'm sure she never wanted to hurt me, Spenser — she's simply sensible enough to know that it's better for two people to be happy than for three to be miserable."

"God save me from sensible women!" he exclaimed violently. "She is ruining your life and mine . . . and Georgina's too, no doubt. Do you expect me to applaud the way she has behaved?"

"She didn't force you into asking Georgina to marry you," Victoria pointed out stubbornly.

"It was entirely due to that little vixen that I proposed to Georgina," he retorted furiously. "Do you suppose I *want* to marry her . . . heaven help me, it's the last thing I want!"

"Then I hope heaven *will* help you for she certainly won't," Victoria said bluntly. "She won't let you slip through her fingers now." She looked at him thoughtfully. "You really do love Sophy, don't you? Oh, what a mess it all is! And it wouldn't help if I refused to divorce Luke, would it?"

"No," he said curtly.

She sighed. "Give me ten minutes to throw some things into a case . . . I will come to Staples with you, Spenser . . . "

She went swiftly from the room and he strode to the window and stood, hands thrust deep into his pockets, contemplating the passing traffic and seeing none of it. He had been surprised that Luke had acted so swiftly . . . the man must be more anxious for his freedom than he had supposed. No doubt Sophy could be very persuasive and he knew only too well that a man could desire her above everything else in the world. Yet he had not really expected to find that Luke had already spoken to Victoria on the subject of divorce.

He grimaced. Divorce was an ugly word and an ugly business . . . it saddened him that it should be threatening his sister and his family name. Chadwicks had always lived with their mistakes and refused to admit defeat, rightly or wrongly . . . and there was no doubt that divorce was a public admission of failure. Their pride would be trampled in the dust, he thought grimly — thanks to Sophy Ransome!

If only he could dismiss her with the contempt she deserved. He had spent a sleepless night trying to whip up his anger and his loathing for the girl who had scorned him for his sister's husband . . . and he had failed miserably. He could not defend her — but he could not deny that he loved her. Without even trying, she had taken complete possession of his heart and mind and the sudden realisation of that fact had brought with it an appalled awareness of the enormity of marrying any woman but the one he loved. Pride and fury had urged him to propose to Georgina . . . and within moments he had been calm enough to realise the stupid and irrevocable step he had taken.

Georgina was cock-a-hoop, of course . . . full of wedding plans and plans for the future to which he had been scarcely able to murmur more than vague agreement. He doubted if she had noticed his lack of enthusiasm . . . or attached much importance to it. Their engagement would be announced shortly and within a month he would be a married man, he thought bitterly. He knew she had expected him to postpone his return to Staples once again but he had pleaded pressure of work and assured her that he would be in town for the inevitable social round by the end of the following week. He needed those few days, he thought desperately . . . time to come to terms with his feeling for Sophy and the knowledge that he must marry Georgina. A man in his position could not jilt any woman . . . his only hope lay in her unlikely change of heart — and that was no hope at all where Georgina was concerned. She meant to marry him — and he did not think that even a confession of his love for Sophy would deter her. He had no intention of confessing it, of course . . . only one woman was entitled to know the innermost secrets of his heart and she would never hear them.

He turned as Victoria came into the room, a coat slung about her shoulders. She looked very pale but determined. "I'm ready," she announced calmly.

"Very well . . . do you mean to leave a message for Luke?"

"I suppose he will have to know

where I am . . . although it must be obvious that I've left town with you. He knows that you are going home this morning." Her glance fell on Luke's note, lying on the breakfast table. She opened her bag and took out the small silver pencil she used to jot notes in her engagement book. Taking up Luke's note she swiftly scribbled a few lines, refolded it and laid it down where she had originally found it when she came down to breakfast.

She was calm only because she was refusing to think about the step she was taking or of Luke's reaction when he discovered that she had left him . . . she did not allow herself to wonder if he would be relieved or regretful. She would not allow herself to hope because despair might follow — and that was already too close to her heart. But Spenser was probably right to carry her off to Staples . . . Luke would know where to find her if he decided that life without her was intolerable, after all — and if he was determined on divorce then she was better off out of town and away from the curiosity and commiseration of her friends.

Luke was able to leave the office earlier than he had anticipated, the last of his appointments cancelled by the illness of a business associate. He drove home, preparing all that he meant to say to Victoria, determined to be kind but resolute, gentle but firmly insistent that if she wanted their marriage to last then she must grant him the respect and the consideration that he merited as her husband.

His confidence ebbed considerably as he brought the car to a standstill outside the house . . . he might be about to alienate Victoria for ever and bring their marriage crashing in ruins.

He walked into the sitting-room where he expected to find her . . . and stopped short at the emptiness of the room. He frowned and then turned abruptly and made his way to her room. It was in considerable disorder, clothes strewn haphazardly across the

206

bed, drawers pulled out and left
. . . nothing unusual where Victoria
was concerned for she had still not
accustomed herself to the fact that she
no longer had a personal maid to follow
in her untidy wake.

Luke was annoyed. It looked as
though she had ignored his note and
rushed off to keep an engagement,
having spent too long over choosing
what she would wear to put away all
that she had rejected.

Then he realised that an evening
gown had been carelessly tossed on
the bed . . . and he was suddenly
anxious. She would not be selecting an
evening dress for a lunch appointment
. . . and his heart missed a beat as
he realised that the chaos was more
indicative of hasty packing. He strode
to the wardrobe where she kept her
cases . . . they were missing. So was
the beautiful leather dressing-case that
he had given her quite recently. He
turned to the dressing-table . . . she
had cleared it of brushes, cosmetics,

perfumes — he suddenly had a vivid mental picture of Victoria sweeping everything into the dressing-case with hasty hands.

He felt sick with apprehension and dismay. She could not have gone — without even a word to him! It was not like Victoria to do such a thing . . . she could hit hard, he knew, but she was not capable of foul blows. She was impulsive and often reckless — but she was more likely to announce her decisions to the world than quietly to plan and then slip away without telling him or anyone else.

Slowly he went down the wide staircase and into the dining-room. His glance went immediately to the mantelpiece where he had placed his note to Victoria . . . it remained where he had left it, unopened and unread.

She could not have missed it . . . she had obviously ignored it. And that was significant in itself. For some reason she had not wanted to know what was in the note . . . had not wanted to be reminded of him, perhaps, he thought bleakly.

Remembering the way she had looked in sleep, innocent and untroubled, a faint smile curving her lovely mouth, it seemed particularly difficult to believe that she had gone to bed knowing that in the morning she would pack and walk out of the house and away from him. Yet every instinct cried out that it was the truth . . . she had left him, cruelly and deliberately. He recalled that they had seen little of each other in the past week and he wondered now if she had been avoiding him, afraid to be with him for any length of time in case she impulsively blurted out her intentions.

He went in search of Mrs. Hallows but that brisk and competent woman, an excellent cook and housekeeper but with very little interest in the personal lives of her employers, could tell him very little. Victoria had come down to breakfast about twenty to ten when Mrs. Hallows was on her way up to tidy the bedrooms. She had thought that someone was at the front door while she was busy in Victoria's room but she supposed that either Victoria or the daily woman had admitted the caller . . . the bell had not rung again and she had heard a man's voice in the dining-room when she passed through the hall on her way back to the kitchen. She had gone to clear the dining-room just after ten and found it empty . . . she had not seen or heard Victoria leave the house and she had not been told what to do about lunch. There was some cold meat and salad and fruit but she had not expected to provide lunch for either Luke or Victoria that day.

Luke thanked her for the information, refused the cold meat and left her, grateful for the woman's complete lack of curiosity and feeling even more disturbed about Victoria's sudden departure. A man had called at the house . . . but which man? It seemed obvious that Victoria had left with him . . . but had it been planned or was it a spur of the moment decision. Very likely the latter for although Victoria was not at all methodical she would scarcely have left her packing to the last minute if she had planned to go away.

He felt a little comforted by the thought . . . perhaps her slumber had been as innocent as he had believed at the time. Perhaps she had not really left him at all . . . merely dashed off on an impulse to visit friends or to relax in the South of France for a few days. She had done it before but never without his knowledge and consent.

He hurried to a telephone and rang three or four of her friends without success before it occurred to him to wonder if Sophy knew anything. She had not known on the previous night or it would have been mentioned but she might have seen or heard from Victoria during the morning . . .

9

SOPHY closed the front door just as the telephone rang. Still in her coat, she picked up the receiver and gave the number and her name.

Without preliminaries, Luke demanded anxiously: "Sophy . . . have you any idea where Victoria might be?"

She was a little surprised. "Victoria? She isn't with me, Luke . . . I haven't seen her today."

"Oh . . . I see . . . "

"What is it, Luke?" she asked swiftly sensing his disappointment.

"I'm not sure," he said hesitantly. "Sophy . . . I'm in a bit of a state. Silly, perhaps . . . but Victoria seems to have packed some things and shot off somewhere. Forgetting to tell me where she was going . . . unless she mentioned it earlier in the week and I can't remember . . . " His words sounded weak in his own ears and he trailed off uncertainly.

"You sound worried, Luke!"

"Yes . . . I am," he said baldly. "I think she's left me, Sophy."

"Left you! Surely not . . . oh, Luke, that isn't possible. She has no reason — she must have left a message for you . . . with Mrs. Hallows, perhaps?"

"No . . . I've already checked on that. She left the house this morning about ten . . . no one saw her go and no one knows who was with her except that it may have been a man who called at the house about that time."

"You didn't see her this morning . . . at breakfast or before that?"

"No . . . she was still in bed when I went out — or so I thought, anyway. I've rung one or two people but no one knows if she had any plans . . . it's damnably embarrassing, Sophy."

"Of course," she agreed sympathetically. "But I'm sure there's a simple explanation. You know how impulsive she is . . . I expect she's rushed off to

213

spend the weekend with friends and forgotten to write a note for you. She'll probably telephone later, full of apologies."

Her tone was reassuring for she simply could not believe that Victoria would walk out on Luke in such fashion. Even if she had ceased to love him she was not capable of deliberate cruelty. Luke was naturally upset and worried . . . and if he had rushed home and tackled Victoria on the subject of her behaviour on the previous night without carefully weighing his words, he might be blaming himself for having angered and antagonised her . . . and if he had then it was an obvious explanation for her impulsive flight. She was certainly young enough to think that it would do Luke a great deal of good to be without her for a few days . . . and even more good to suffer all the anguish of not knowing where she was. It was neither kind nor sensible — but Victoria could be both wilful and foolish when she lost her temper.

Sophy didn't doubt that she would regret her action when she calmed down and immediately contact Luke with an explanation and an apology.

Luke desperately needed reassurance but for once Sophy failed him. He thought resentfully that she didn't realise how obvious it was that Victoria had gone and did not mean to come back . . . and then reminded himself that Sophy had not seen the state of Victoria's room or that deserted top of her dressing-table.

"You may be right," he said slowly, his tone completely lacking in conviction.

"Have you tried Spenser . . . he might know where she is," Sophy suggested. She had a little trouble in uttering the name for she was struggling hard to keep him out of her thoughts.

"He'll be on his way to Staples . . . I rang his club but he booked out early this morning."

She could not keep the surprise from her voice as she exclaimed: "Booked out? But surely he hasn't left town now . . . I mean — you've heard the news of his engagement, I suppose? It hasn't been formally announced yet but it's all over town."

"I haven't heard," he said without interest. "Georgina Winslow, I gather?"

"Yes, of course," she returned impatiently. "So he may not have left for Staples at all . . . it would be a little odd, wouldn't it? They only became engaged last night."

"Well, I don't know where to reach him if he is still in town . . . and ten to one he wouldn't know anything about Victoria, anyway. I'll ring round a few more places and let you know if I find out anything."

The telephone clicked in her ear and Sophy replaced her own receiver. She wandered into the sitting-room and sank down into a chair. It had not been a very pleasant morning . . . everyone she had met had been agog with the news of Spenser Chadwick's engagement and it had not been easy for her to exclaim and wonder as though she was

216

as superficially affected as her friends.

Her heart was very heavy. It had seemed a simple thing on the previous night to declare that he must not be allowed to marry a woman like Georgina Winslow and that she must act swiftly before any formal announcement of the engagement could be made. In the cold light of day she could not believe that her impulsive idea would be acceptable to him — or even to herself. She did not lack the courage but she shrank from the despair and frustration she would feel if he refused . . . as he surely would, she thought bleakly.

It was such a brazen thing to do . . . but perhaps he would understand and forgive and let her down lightly if she could convince him that she was solely concerned for his happiness . . .

The telephone shrilled again, interrupting her thoughts. She hurried to answer it and scarcely had time to give the number before Luke blurted furiously: "She's with Marlowe . . . she's gone away with him!"

"Oh, nonsense! I don't believe it!" she refuted immediately.

"It's true . . . it must be! He left London this morning — and took Victoria with him!"

"Who says so?" she demanded. "Spenser?"

"I haven't spoken to him . . . he *has* gone down to Staples. I rang Georgina Winslow," he said impatiently.

"Did she tell you that Victoria is with Julius Marlowe?"

"Of course not . . . I didn't tell *her* that I was anxious to find Victoria. I rang his studio and Sally Bazil told me that Marlowe had gone into the country this morning . . . it's obvious that he is the man who called at the house and persuaded Victoria to pack in such a hurry."

"It isn't obvious to me," she told him firmly. "Victoria isn't such a fool . . . she wouldn't throw everything away for a man like Marlowe. He isn't free to marry her, for one thing — and wouldn't marry her if he was! Luke, you can't believe this impossible thing . . . it can only be coincidence that he's gone out of London today."

"You're very sweet, Sophy," he said wearily. "I admire your loyalty but I think it's misplaced. Victoria has always taken what she wanted without giving a damn for the consequences . . . and at the moment she wants Marlowe. Well, I won't stand in her way — I shall be instructing my solicitors today. It will be up to Victoria to see that he does marry her when they are both free to do so . . . and I imagine his wife won't delay in starting divorce proceedings."

"Luke, you don't know Victoria very well, I'm afraid," she said ruefully.

"So it seems!" he retorted grimly. "I didn't know she was capable of this kind of thing!"

"She isn't! She is much too proud to expose herself to so much unpleasantness — and she wouldn't drag her name through the divorce courts in this way."

"You forget that her name is no

219

longer Chadwick," he reminded her coldly. "She wouldn't hesitate to drag *my* name in the mud . . . I'm not a member of your English aristocracy, after all — just a jumped-up American citizen of Middle European parentage."

"Don't be silly!" she exclaimed, more sharply than she had ever spoken to him. "Don't *wallow*, Luke — it's bad enough that you're so ready to believe the worst of poor Victoria! I thought you loved her!"

"So did I!" he snapped. "But I only loved a figment of my imagination, it seems . . . I never knew the real woman. She never allowed me to know her!"

"If you mean to talk like that then I'm not prepared to help," she said bluntly.

"What can *you* do?" he demanded roughly.

"I don't know . . . yet. But I shall find Victoria and prove to you how mistaken you are to judge her without a smattering of real evidence!"

"I hope you may . . . and I hope she has a very good explanation for walking out on me without a word!"

She forgave him readily for slamming down the receiver . . . he was anxious and upset and furiously blaming himself that Victoria had been unhappy enough to leave him. Whereas Sophy was much inclined to blame herself . . . for if she had left him to sort things out for himself from the beginning none of this might have happened. He had been troubled and bewildered and she had given him what she believed to be good advice . . . but now she wondered if Victoria had looked for an opposition that indicated concern rather than a patient tolerance which might imply an indifference to her wayward behaviour.

She should have known better than to interfere in their matrimonial problems, she thought ruefully . . . she had probably done much more harm than good and it was no excuse that she had only been trying to help.

She still did not know if Luke had spoken to Victoria on the previous night . . . but it was possible that they had quarrelled. It would explain why he had merely left her a note when he left the house instead of going up to her room to speak to her . . . and it would also explain Victoria's impetuous decision to accompany Spenser to Staples.

For she had been suddenly convinced that she would find Victoria at Staples. Spenser was not likely to leave town without bidding his sister good-bye . . . and he might well be the man who had called at the house that morning. In fact, the more she thought about it the more likely it seemed that he had called on Victoria . . . not only to say good-bye but to tell her of his engagement to Georgina Winslow.

Victoria was very proud. However willing she might be to end her association with Julius Marlowe at her husband's insistence she would have found it difficult to submit meekly to his authority. How much easier it must have seemed to her to go away for a while and allow her friendship with Julius to wither for want of encouragement rather than make the clean break that Luke demanded and which might excite comment.

Spenser was going home at a convenient moment and she could travel with him. Angry with Luke, she had impulsively decided not to let him know where she was going . . . let him worry about her for a few days and perhaps he would be sorry for his harsh words.

It was in character, Sophy thought . . . and Victoria could not have known that Marlowe was planning to leave town the same day. It must be the last thing she would want to have Luke or anyone else suspect that they had gone away together.

Unfortunately, Luke would not be the only one to leap to that ridiculous conclusion as soon as it became known that both Marlowe and Victoria were out of town . . . and particularly when

Luke seemed so set on betraying his ignorance of her whereabouts. Although there was no foundation for the gossip it would be very harmful . . . and so it was imperative that Victoria should be persuaded to return to London and to Luke at the earliest possible moment . . .

Within a very short time, Sophy was threading her way through the busy traffic, en route for Staples. She had paused only to thrust a few things for the night into a small case for she did not anticipate returning to London until the following day and to change into a suit that would serve her for the journey and for the evening she must spend at Staples.

She was looking forward to seeing the place for the first time, having heard so much about its beauties . . . she only wished she could visit it in happier circumstances.

Victoria might resent her interference and refuse to be dragged back to town like a naughty child . . . but she would have to be persuaded. Perhaps that marriage was doomed to failure no matter what she did but at least it could be ended with dignity and discretion.

It was odd that circumstances were taking her to the very man that she most wished to avoid for the time being . . . it was almost as though fate was forcing her into confronting him with the proposition that had kept her awake most of the night. For she knew that she could not meet him without speaking her mind no matter what humiliation she invited . . .

Once she left London and its suburbs behind she made good time on the road . . . and lost a little of it in finding Staples which was set deep in the heart of country that was unknown to her.

Her heart was a little unsteady as she mounted the wide stone steps and wielded the heavy antique knocker that decorated the massive front door. She had time to observe the magnificence of the old Hall and to appreciate the beauty of its formal gardens before the door was opened. She had expected a servant of some sort and was not prepared for the sight of Spenser . . . and she stepped back in confusion.

He stared at her incredulously, convinced that his tired brain was playing tricks on him. Then she smiled . . . a tentative little smile which implied that she was not certain of her reception. He looked from her slender figure to the car parked in the drive and then back again. His hand moved impulsively towards her and he said violently: "What the devil are *you* doing here?"

That instinctive movement of his hand went unnoticed in the impact of those forceful words. The colour rushed to her face. But she rallied quickly. "Why, Spenser . . . you invited me to spend a weekend," she told him lightly. "Have you forgotten? You promised to show me over the estate."

His eyes narrowed. He had not thought her capable of such audacity . . . and he could not imagine what had really brought her to Staples at this particular time. "You'd better drive back to London," he said roughly. "You are not welcome here."

Sophy felt as though he had slapped her face. The words were so unexpected . . . she racked her brain for an explanation of his hostility for they had parted on amicable terms at their last meeting and she could not understand the anger and the contempt that were so evident in his voice.

Her temper flared abruptly. "Very well . . . but I came to talk to Victoria and I don't mean to leave until I've done so."

He laughed . . . an angry, mocking laugh. "Proud words . . . but you'll find that Victoria will not see you. You can say nothing that she will want to hear."

"She may tell me that herself," Sophy said firmly. "If I may come in . . .?"

He shrugged. "I suppose you must," he said coldly, stepping back to allow her to enter the vast, panelled hall with its wide, curving staircase. Sophy wished she was in the mood to appreciate her surroundings but she merely gave them a cursory glance of appraisal and turned again to the man whose expression was so forbidding. "Victoria is in her room. I'll tell her that you are here if you insist — but I promise you that you've wasted a journey." He turned on his heel and strode towards the staircase.

Sophy looked after him, struggling with her pain and her pride. "Spenser . . . !" she exclaimed involuntarily.

He paused and turned to look at her, an eyebrow raised in cool query. There was so much arrogance in his attitude that her heart sank . . . how foolish she had been to indulge in those wild dreams, to suppose that he would ever listen to her proposal let alone consider it. It was so obvious that he disliked and despised her . . . and she had almost persuaded herself that he was not entirely indifferent to her even if he did plan to marry another woman . . .

"What have I done?" she asked quietly, deploring her own weakness but knowing the importance of trying to thrust through that strange and bewildering barrier. "You didn't seem to hate me so the last time we met."

He was furious that she should remind him of the moment which was so often in his thoughts — the moment when she had stood in his embrace and received his kiss with such unflattering composure. "I didn't know you for what you are — then!" he snapped. "I was foolish enough to be deceived by you — to like and respect you then!"

The venom in his tone made her catch her breath and she felt the blood draining from her cheeks. Her eyes were very large and shocked in her small, pale face but she met his cold gaze with steadiness. "I never tried to deceive you, Spenser," she said quietly.

"In all fairness you should tell me how I've offended you."

"I advise you to search your conscience — if you possess such a thing!" he retorted grimly.

"My conscience is perfectly clear," she replied carefully, struggling to suppress her own surging temper. "I hope yours may be if you leave me to stand here as though I were a servant! Indeed, you would not treat a servant so casually, I daresay!"

"You are quite right, Sophy — he spoils them dreadfully," Victoria said lightly from the head of the staircase. "Spenser, what are you thinking of? Sophy must have been driving for hours and looks quite exhausted — you mustn't be so unkind." She ran down the stairs, sending her brother a swift reproachful glance. "Come into the sitting-room, Sophy — and Spenser will order some tea for you."

Sophy looked at Spenser's wrathful countenance and, hurt and angry though she felt, she could not help the mischief leaping to her eyes. "I hope he may not poison it," she said lightly.

Without the slightest flicker of response, he turned on his heel . . . and Sophy allowed her friend to draw her into the comfortable room which was ablaze with the rays of the evening sun. She could not believe that it was anything more than some foolish misunderstanding which had led Spenser to react so violently to her arrival . . . she knew that she was innocent of any word or act that could have invoked his lasting enmity. For the moment she must concentrate on the reason for her visit to Staples . . . later she must surely have an opportunity to unravel the mystery of Spenser's attitude . . .

Victoria had been astonished to hear Sophy's voice in the hall when she came out of her room. Like her brother, she could not imagine why she should come to Staples at this particular time until it occurred to her that her sudden flight might have been interpreted as a refusal to even discuss the possibility of a divorce with Luke. Perhaps he and Sophy believed that she meant to throw every obstacle in their path to happiness and so Sophy had decided to follow her to Staples in order to plead with her.

It might astonish Spenser that she did not share his anger and contempt for Sophy. But she was staunch in her affections and she found it impossible to blame her friend. She knew that she alone was to blame for the failure of her marriage . . . it could have been both happy and successful if she had behaved differently from the beginning. She thought it very natural that Luke should have turned to someone as warmly loving and generous as Sophy — and she knew in her heart that Sophy had not deliberately tried to end a marriage which had delighted her so much when it took place. If she was prepared to sacrifice their friendship for the sake of the happiness she and Luke could know then it must be because she was deeply in love with Luke. The only sacrifice must be her own ... and her only comfort the knowledge that Luke at least would be happier than he had been since she married him ...

"I know why you're here," she said slowly, trying to keep a tremor from her voice. "You've come to plead with me ... but you need not. Luke's happiness is all that matters to me, Sophy — I wish he might have found it with me but I know it's my fault that he didn't. You will make him happy — and that's all I want, truly."

Sophy stared at her in blank astonishment — and wondered if this was one of those dreams where everyone but herself made sense of the situation. "Are you giving Luke to *me*?" she demanded in amazement.

Victoria nodded. "I won't stand in your way, I promise you."

"*My* way ... but this is absurd!

I don't want Luke," Sophy protested indignantly.

Victoria smiled at her . . . it was a sweet, rueful smile. "He hasn't spoken to you yet, then . . . but I suppose he wouldn't until everything was settled. Sophy, you don't have to pretend with me . . . not now. I know you love each other — and I'm not angry with either of you. These things happen . . . they aren't planned. I know you didn't mean to hurt me . . ."

"Victoria . . . be quiet and listen to me!" Sophy said sharply. "I'm *not* in love with Luke . . . it's never occurred to me to even think of him in that way. I don't know where you got such a ridiculous idea! Luke and I . . . ! Why, it's nonsense! The sun shines out of your eyes as far as he's concerned and you're a fool if you doubt it!"

Victoria shook her head sadly. "Please don't lie to me, Sophy . . . I can't bear it just now. Luke wants a divorce and I'm willing to give him his freedom . . . it can be done quietly and without fuss or scandal and then you can be married and be happy."

"A noble sacrifice . . . but quite unnecessary," Sophy said firmly. "Heaven knows why you should suppose that Luke wants to be rid of you . . . but I can assure you that you're mistaken. He is quite frantic with worry about you. You really are an impetuous idiot, Victoria — to run off like that simply because of a silly quarrel!"

Victoria looked up swiftly, startled. "There was no quarrel!"

"Then why on earth did you do it? What possessed you? You may not know that Julius Marlowe also left town this morning but I suppose it won't surprise you that Luke believes you to be with him!"

Victoria leaped to her feet. "But why? I told him where I was going . . . I left him a note!" She searched Sophy's face in almost frantic dismay. "How could he believe such a thing?"

235

"I imagine it was quite easy in the circumstances," Sophy said dryly. "You've been flaunting the man in Luke's face long enough. Did you really leave a note?"

"Yes, of course I did," Victoria retorted indignantly.

"Well, he didn't see it . . . not before I left town anyway. I came down here to persuade you to go back with me before the whole of London is convinced that you've run off with Marlowe . . . and that is the kind of scandal you can well do without, Victoria. Ring Luke now and let him know where you are, for heaven's sake . . . I only hope he thought better of rushing off to his solicitor this afternoon!"

Victoria stared at her bleakly. "He was in a hurry to start proceedings . . . and you claim that he doesn't want a divorce!"

"Of course he doesn't . . . but he's as noble as you are and is determined not to stand in the way of your happiness." An involuntary little chuckle escaped her and Victoria glared at her indignantly. "Oh, I'm sorry . . . it isn't a laughing matter, I know. But if only you two would stop being so noble and self-sacrificing and admit that you can't be happy without each other . . . and you still haven't told me why you suspected *me* of wanting to marry Luke!"

"People have been talking . . . you do see each other quite a lot, don't you?" Victoria said slowly.

"If you neglect your husband you shouldn't be surprised if he turns to his friends for comfort and advice," Sophy said bluntly.

Victoria coloured faintly. "I ought to have known you better, of course . . . I didn't want to believe the gossip but I knew I'd been a bad wife to Luke and I could understand that he might prefer you to me. Then Spenser came and seemed to know all about Luke's plans for a divorce and he was so angry with *you* . . . "

Interrupting her, Sophy said slowly, her green eyes glittering with fury: "Spenser knew all about it, did he . . . such perception and intelligence is astonishing! Naturally he knew that I'm just the woman to take advantage of our friendship so that I could steal your husband! I'm obliged to him!"

10

SPENSER lay back in a deep armchair, hands behind his head, his gaze fixed unseeingly on a family portrait that adorned the library wall.

He was engaged in a fierce battle with his heart and his honour. Every fibre of his being cried out against the marriage he had proposed to a woman he did not love. Even though he would never possess Sophy it was intolerable to him to contemplate a future with Georgina by his side — his wife, the mistress of Staples, the mother of his children.

Perhaps if he did not love Sophy so much . . . but in his heart he knew that if she did not exist, if they had never met, he could never have sacrificed himself to his duty in this way . . . bind himself to a woman who meant nothing to him merely for the sake of an heir. He would never have asked Georgina to marry him if he had not been so furious with Sophy, so desperately hurt and so bitterly disappointed by her lack of integrity.

He must break the engagement which was no more than a farce and would surely lead to a tragic unhappiness for them both if they married without love or mutual desire or even more than ordinary liking. He was thankful that Georgina was not particularly fond of him . . . her pride would suffer badly but her heart would not.

He could not delay matters — at the moment their engagement was unofficial and might be ended without exposing her to too much humiliation. He had specifically requested her not to spread the news until he had seen her father on the following day and a formal announcement could be made . . . if she had made the mistake of telling her friends then she would only have herself to blame.

He was a very proud man and he prided himself on being a careful guardian of his family name. It was bad enough that in the near future his sister would smear it with the stigma of the first divorce in the family . . . could he really dishonour it even more by refusing to marry a woman who had accepted him in good faith?

There was no alternative, he decided. It would be more dishonourable to marry Georgina when he was deeply in love with another woman.

On that decision, he reached for the telephone — a cowardly way to deal her such a blow, he knew, but delay would not improve matters. By the time he could reach London the following day she might have told more of her friends that she was going to marry him . . . if the news was already circulating then it was vital that it should be scotched as a rumour as soon as possible and Georgina would be glad to do it to save her face.

It was fortunate that he found her at

home but the next ten minutes were the most difficult of his life. It took some time to convince Georgina that he was in earnest. She was angry and then accusing . . . he had expected the one but not the other and it was a shock to discover that she was already aware of his feeling for Sophy. He could not allow her to abuse the woman he loved and so he was forced to defend Sophy, angry though he was with the girl who had hurt him so much and sorely threatened his sister's happiness. It was not easy for him to admit that his love for someone else prevented him from marrying the woman who had accepted his proposal only the previous evening — and he thought grimly that Georgina would probably delight in spreading that admission all over town. Sophy would inevitably come to hear of it . . . and his fury rose at the thought of her amusement. He could not even suppose that she would be gratified to know that she had won his love without even trying . . . he knew too well in what contempt she held him!

Eventually Georgina slammed the receiver back into its cradle with a violence that hurt his ear. Appalled by the venomous spite of her last words, Spenser slowly replaced his own receiver and knew a heartfelt relief that he had resolved to tell her the truth. He could imagine the kind of life she would have led him if he had foolishly married her only to inadvertently betray his love for Sophy. Georgina might not love him but she would not tolerate his desire for another woman. Hell hath no fury, he thought grimly . . . and wondered how much harm Georgina could do to Sophy's reputation if she carried out her angry threats. Then he remembered Sophy was bent on ruining her own reputation and the sickness of despair rose in him once more.

He had left Victoria and Sophy to their tête-à-tête. He was out of patience with his sister who insisted on regarding Sophy as though she was about to grant her a valuable favour . . . and he could not trust himself within sight or sound of Sophy.

He wondered ruefully how he had come to be in such thrall to a girl who could behave as she had. How was it possible for him to love her so much, to desire her so fiercely, to feel that life without her would be empty and bleak and worthless? Did Luke experience this fierce and compelling need for a woman who was not his wife? If so, then Spenser felt he could understand why Luke could contemplate the breaking of Victoria's heart without a qualm. If he could believe that there was the slightest chance of possessing Sophy he would gladly sacrifice the world and everyone in it to gain his happiness. She was an enchantress. She had bewitched him entirely. One glance from her mischievous green eyes had proved to be the arrow of desire that could penetrate the armour which had always protected his heart.

He had not chosen to love her . . . he had been so convinced that love was just a word. Love . . . it seemed such a small and inadequate word for the emotion which possessed his entire being, for the relentless need which she had inspired and which he had tried so hard to ignore and deny. Such a small word . . . yet what other word was there to encompass the yearning and the tenderness, the aching need, the desperate desire to give himself utterly to the securing of her happiness, her contentment, her welfare and security. He wanted to give her the world and all it contained — at the same time he wanted to wring her neck for bringing him to this pass where all that mattered was the longing to have and to hold one woman to his heart until death did them part . . .

The sound of a car interrupted his reverie. At first he supposed it to be Sophy on her way back to town and he rose instinctively to his feet with the need to speak to her once more before she left. He had not expected her to stay at Staples after the rough reception she had received at his hands but the thought that she could leave without exchanging another word with him wrenched at his heart.

Then he realised that it was the sound of a car approaching the house. He strode to the open window which overlooked the drive . . . and discovered in some surprise that it was Luke behind the wheel of the car.

Luke braked and swung the car to a standstill with all the urgency of a man who brooked no delay in his errand. There was grim determination in the set of his mouth as he stepped from the car and strode towards the house.

Spenser moved swiftly to the door and out into the hall. The heavy knocker resounded throughout the house as Luke wielded it with energy and determination.

But his effort was quite unnecessary. For Victoria was already on her way across the hall, her eyes shining . . . and she threw open the heavy door and greeted her husband with a smile that spoke volumes.

Luke looked at her for a long moment . . . then, satisfied with all that he saw in her lovely face, he drew her into his arms with a deep sigh and they clung together as though they would never release each other again.

Spenser turned away, reluctant to intrude on that moment when it was so obvious to him that nothing mattered to those two but their need for each other. He did not know how the misunderstanding had arisen but there was nothing wrong with that marriage that Luke and Victoria could not sort out for themselves, he thought thankfully.

He paused as a slight movement caught his eye . . . Sophy had come to the open door of the sitting-room and she stood very still, looking at that touching tableau with a hint of wistful sadness in her green eyes. Then sensing his gaze, she looked up and at him.

Her eyes and mouth hardened abruptly and he took a step towards her, about to speak her name. She shook her head instinctively and retreated into the sitting-room . . . and, respecting the emotions which he believed to possess her, he did not follow her. Instead he turned on his heel and re-entered the library, closing the door with a little snap of finality.

Sophy was not alone for long. Luke was the first to come back to reality. He kissed his wife lightly on the nose and she smiled up at him happily. "Darling idiot . . . I don't know why you ran off like that but it doesn't really seem to matter now. I've been in a terrible state . . . I thought you'd gone away with Marlowe until I discovered your shocking scrawl at the bottom of my note. I've come to take you home, Victoria."

She nodded. "Sophy came for the same reason . . . I was just about to telephone you when I heard the car. Oh, Luke, I've been such a fool . . . "

He silenced her with a kiss. "Perhaps we both have, my sweet. Sophy is here, did you say?"

"Yes . . . she guessed I'd be here with Spenser. She was afraid that everyone would think I'd left town with Julius. She said I must go home and straighten things out with you . . . and once I realised that you didn't want her and it was all a crazy mix-up on my part I knew that it was the only thing I wanted to do." She drew him towards the sitting-room. "We must tell Sophy that you are here . . . I rushed out of the room like a demented hen when I heard the car. She must be wondering what's happened."

"Sophy knows what's happened . . . and I couldn't be more pleased to see you," Sophy said lightly, catching the tail end of her friend's words as they entered the room. "I told you it was time you took her in hand, Luke . . . she was so sure that you didn't care what she did that she managed to convince herself that you'd fallen out of love with her and was planning to run off with me. She really does need a keeper, I'm afraid."

"She needs me," he said firmly, smiling down at his wife. "And I shall see to it that she doesn't dream up any more cockeyed ideas for getting rid of me." Sliding an arm about her waist he drew Victoria close. "You've got me for life, my sweet — so reconcile yourself to the thought."

"I shall never want anyone else," she said softly . . . and raised herself on her toes to kiss him.

Sophy slipped from the room, feeling a very unnecessary third. She was thankful that they had settled their differences so swiftly and so simply . . . yet she could not help envying their delight in each other and it hurt too much to witness it any longer.

Quietly she made her way to the front door, meaning to slip from the house without a word to anyone. She did not think that she would even be missed . . . and certainly there was no place for her beneath this roof. Luke and Victoria wanted no one but each other . . . and Spenser had made it very clear that he resented her very presence at Staples. She did not expect to reach London that night . . . it was already growing late. But there were plenty of hotels on her route . . .

Spenser came out into the hall just as she reached the door. He moved swiftly towards her and she turned at the sound of his footsteps. "Sophy!" he said sharply as she turned back to struggle with the difficult latch of the door.

She looked at him briefly over her shoulder and he was startled by the blazing anger in those green eyes. "Well?" she demanded coldly.

"You are not leaving?" he asked, a little foolishly when it was so obvious what she was doing.

"I am indeed," she told him with a tilt of her chin. "You were right . . . I wasted my journey — but I didn't know Luke would follow me, you see."

"It's getting late . . . you cannot drive all the way back to town tonight," he protested.

"No . . . but I shall find somewhere to spend the night. I am not welcome in this house . . . and would not stay if I were!"

"Come — you are being silly," he said gently. "I spoke in anger and you know it. I didn't really mean all I said to you, Sophy. Forgive me?" He put out his hand to her, wanting only in that moment to offer some comfort, knowing how she must be feeling.

She ignored the gesture and fumbled again with the catch of the door. She was trembling with fury and pain that he had found it so easy to think ill of her. Yet the unexpected tenderness of his tone had brought swift and exceedingly foolish tears to her eyes and she dared not let him see their wetness.

He covered her hand with his own. "Don't go just yet then . . . someone owes me an explanation and *they* have forgotten the existence of everyone but themselves," he said, nodding his head in the direction of the room where Luke and Victoria were still locked in each other's arms.

Wrenching her hand away from his touch, she turned on him with such a blaze in her eyes that he stepped back involuntarily. "But you know it all — you know that Luke and I are so much in love that we've been carrying on an affair for weeks behind Victoria's back — that he is so desperate to marry me that he wants a divorce and that I'm so steeped in iniquity that I won't hesitate to trample on Victoria's feelings in order to get what I want! You know all that — what more do you want to know?"

"I knew nothing . . . merely leaped to what was evidently the wrong conclusion," he said quietly, reasonably. "It seems that Victoria has exaggerated my part in this business. She was very upset this morning because she believed Luke wanted his freedom so that he could marry you ... *I* didn't put that into her head, I assure you. I brought her here to protect her from the unpleasantness she would suffer if it was true ... and I believed it to be true, I admit."

"Of course — you knew *me* so well!" she flared.

"I knew you loved Luke," he said with a calmness that did not betray his difficulty in uttering the words. "I saw you together last night ... I believed you were urging him to ask Victoria for a divorce."

"You saw us together — and knew immediately that I loved Luke! How transparent I must be ... or how frighteningly perceptive you are!" she said scathingly.

He thought he understood her anger. She was suffering — and in her pain she had to lash out at someone. He knew that feeling only too well. He did not mind bearing the brunt of her anguish ... it was little enough he could do for her. "There were — other reasons for that belief," he said slowly. "But my mistake was in supposing that you would take what you wanted and damn the consequences. I have maligned you, Sophy . . . I should have realised that you are too generous to hurt anyone."

"Even if I knew that Luke was too happy with his wife to want me? Very generous of me to sacrifice a happiness I knew I could never have!" she threw at him coldly.

"You must know that you could have Luke or any other man if you wanted him enough," he told her, a little harshly.

She stared at him in surprise at the words. Then she laughed . . . and it was a bleak little laugh. "You must think I'm irresistible!" she exclaimed wryly.

"I think you have the gift of inspiring love — if you choose," he told her quietly. "I think you know that Luke would love you if you allowed it to happen . . . and I admire your courage in surrendering him at the cost of your own happiness."

"Don't credit me with so much nobility!" Sophy cried, carried beyond caution by a sudden *volte face* of her emotions. From angry determination that he should never suspect how much he meant to her to a fierce desire to rid him of the foolish misapprehension that she cared for Luke took but a moment . . . and she did not care if she betrayed the way she felt about him. There was something in his eyes, in his voice, in the still tension of his tall body that caused her to wonder with a violent leap of her heart if his angry contempt had been born of jealousy rather than the belief that she sought to destroy his sister's happiness. Was it possible that he had liked and admired her more than she had known or dreamed? Was it possible that his engagement to Georgina Winslow would never have happened if he had not seen her with Luke and leaped to an idiotic conclusion? Her chin tilted suddenly as she looked up at him and she added impulsively, breathlessly: "I didn't come just to see Victoria, you know . . . I also wanted to see you — to ask you to marry me!"

The impact of her words seemed to drive the breath from his own body. He stared at her in astonishment . . . and she looked back at him with something very like defiance in her eyes — defiance and something else he did not choose at that moment to define. For he must not be too swift to suppose that she meant those astounding words — or could have the best reason in the world for uttering them.

Abruptly he took her arm in a grip that was painful but she made no effort to shake off his hand. "We can't talk here," he said roughly. "Come into the library . . . I want a drink — and I want an explanation that can't be overheard by the entire household."

Sophy allowed him to lead her into the quiet, book-lined room. Outwardly she was calm and self-possessed . . . but her heart was hammering and her pulses racing and her throat threatened to close in panic. She stole a glance at him and was dismayed by the grimness of his expression. He probably felt grim, she thought bleakly, having had those words thrown at his head by a girl he scarcely knew . . . but it was too late to retract them and she must explain herself — at the same time making it clear that nothing would induce her to marry him now even if by some miracle he should wish it . . .

She sank into a chair as he released her. He closed the door firmly and walked across the room to the decanters that stood on a side table. He poured her a drink and carried the glass to her and she took it without really wanting it. He leaned against the edge of the heavy desk that dominated the room and looked down at her, unsmiling, taut and very determined.

She found it impossible to meet his eyes. She sipped the fiery liquid in her glass and almost choked. "I don't drink whisky!" she protested involuntarily, sending him a reproachful glance.

He smiled faintly. "You do now," he told her in a voice that brooked no argument. "I think you're going to need it — for I won't be palmed off with anything but the truth, Sophy. Drink it — and then tell me what you meant by that astonishing statement."

"It isn't going to be easy to explain," she admitted, a little ruefully.

"Oh, I don't think you lack for courage," he said carelessly. "Or candour . . . as I've already discovered on several occasions. You really are a most outrageous person, Sophy Ransome."

She smiled for the first time, relieved by the hint of laughter in his voice. "I know," she agreed honestly. "Things that are in my mind just leap out on my tongue."

"Then it *was* in your mind . . . proposing marriage to me, I mean?"

She nodded — and looked at him

with a gleam of mischief in her eyes. "Oh yes ... I drove all the way from town nerving myself to pop the question," she said lightly.

"To be greeted by a raging fiend — naturally you changed your mind on the instant," he suggested with a smile that warmed her heart.

"Naturally," she agreed — and now her eyes were dancing. She still had every reason to be angry with him but it was impossible for her to ignore the humour in the situation.

Thoughtfully he studied the amber liquid in his own glass. "Of course you were not aware that I became engaged to Georgina Winslow last night."

"Yes, I was ... I saw you with her last night — have you forgotten? I can also draw conclusions, Spenser — but mine had more basis in fact. I already knew that you were looking for a wife — and why. You've been dating Georgina heavily and last night I knew she'd got what she wanted."

He looked at her with narrowed eyes.

"But you didn't believe it was what I wanted?"

"No, I didn't," she said frankly. "So I knew I had to see you before it was too late — and coming after Victoria was all the excuse I needed to come to Staples. I guessed she would be here when I heard that you'd left town — and it seemed to me that if you'd rushed away so soon after getting engaged then you must be very anxious to escape the immediate results. You don't really want to marry Georgina, do you?"

It was more of a statement than a question and he was surprised by her bluntness. But he was amused by the directness of her approach. "Perhaps not . . . but you are aware that I need an heir," he pointed out, his eyes twinkling.

"Yes — and if you married me I could give you one," she said calmly.

He raised a quizzical eyebrow. "Is this the same girl who declared that she would never undertake a marriage

261

of convenience?" he asked mockingly.

The colour stole softly into her face but she returned coolly enough: "I also told you that I didn't suffer from a surfeit of pride, Spenser."

"Very true . . . but it still puzzles me that you should want to marry me," he said lightly.

"You have a great deal to offer . . . and I think I should enjoy being a countess," she returned promptly.

He looked down at her steadily . . . and she lowered her own gaze in some confusion. His smile deepened and a warm glow of satisfaction began to encompass his heart. He had scarcely dared to hope that she might care for him but her answer, whether she knew it or not, was a betrayal that delighted him. For he knew instinctively that Sophy was not a woman to marry for such a reason. "So although you knew I'd already chosen a bride you decided to nominate yourself for the rôle . . . may I ask why?"

"You'd hate being married to

Georgina . . . you aren't at all suited," she said bluntly.

"Not a very good answer, Sophy," he said quietly. "You've had time to think of a much more convincing reply to that question."

She leaned forward and carefully placed the unfinished drink on the desk: "I want you to be happy . . . and Georgina will make you utterly miserable, I know," she replied quietly, looking everywhere but at those dancing, mocking eyes.

"And you believe that you can make me happy?" he asked gently, reaching for her hand and imprisoning it between his strong fingers.

She met his eyes and this time she did not flinch from the steadiness of his grey gaze. "Do I seem to be abominably conceited, Spenser?" she asked ruefully. "You see, I do believe that I can make you happy. I can make you laugh, for one thing — and that is important. Georgina has no sense of humour, I'm told."

263

"But you also exasperate me very much," he pointed out, smiling.

"I know," she admitted. "But I'd try not to . . . and you would find me very adaptable. I've had to be — following the drum with my father all these years." She rose impulsively to her feet and moved closer to him. "Wouldn't you prefer to have me instead of Georgina?" she asked with a tiny catch in her voice.

He longed to enfold her in his arms and hold her against his heart. But he would not rush that magical moment . . . perhaps it was a little unkind to tease her in this way but it was a joy to him to see the delicious colour stealing into her face and to see the unexpected shyness in her eyes and to know that all the warm and generous wealth in her nature was offered to him so freely and so gladly.

His thumb moved in a slow caress over the velvety texture of her wrist and he smiled down at her small face with tenderness and understanding in his eyes. "I couldn't allow you to sacrifice yourself in such a way, Sophy," he said softly. ·

Panic assailed her swiftly. "Oh, it isn't a sacrifice!" she exclaimed urgently. "I'd like to marry you!"

"Because you want to be a countess," he said, challenging her.

At last she recognised the teasing in his voice . . . and allowed herself to believe the loving tenderness in his smile. A tremulous little smile curved her own lips and with her free hand she reached out tentatively to touch his cheek. "Because I love you," she said simply.

Satisfied and aware that this was only the beginning of a happiness he had never expected to know, Spenser drew her gently into his arms . . . and in the sweetness of her lips he found all the response and reassurance of a love that matched his own . . .